DISAPPEARANCE ON ROUTE 6

ASHLEY BUNDY

Disappearance on Route 6

Copyright 01/05/2025, by Ashley Bundy.

This book is a work of fiction. Names, characters, places, and incidents are either the product of the author's imagination or are used fictitiously. Any resemblance to actual persons, living or dead, or actual events or locales is entirely coincidental. This book, both in its entirety and in portions, is the sole property of Ashley Bundy.

Disappearance on Route 6 Copyright © 2025 by Ashley Bundy all rights reserved, including the right to reproduce this book, or any portions thereof, in any form. No part of this text may be reproduced, transmitted, downloaded, decompiled, reverse engineered, or stored in or introduced into any information storage and retrieval system, in any form or by any means, whether electronic or mechanical, without the express permission of the author. The scanning, uploading, and distribution of this book via the internet or any other means without the permission of the publisher is illegal and punishable by law. The only exception is by a reviewer, who may quote short excerpts in a review.

Cover by D.E Hyde Cover Designs

Also by Ashley Bundy

The Blackwood Manor Duology

Blackwood Manor
The Haven Stone

For Don.
Because real life is constant trouble.

Susanna-1996

Susanna Patterson drove along the dark road at a steady pace with her high beams on. She could barely see ten feet ahead of her as an overwhelming darkness surrounded her, devouring everything in its path. A relentless and unyielding chill crept down her spine as soon as she found herself lost. She'd been so tired that she'd exited the highway early without thinking and hadn't even realized it at first.

She'd noted how she saw less and less on the road, as it narrowed. She'd turned off when she saw buildings awhile back, hoping to find food for the kids but the buildings were abandoned. Now she was in the middle of nowhere, somewhere in Virginia. She needed to get to the nearest town, put the kids to bed, and recharge. She would find some way to get back on track in the morning.

The car shuddered, stalling with a grind and a coughing exhaust.

Susanna closed her eyes, sighed in frustration, muttered *"Are you kidding me?"* to herself, took a deep breath, and tried to turn the ignition again.

Click. Click. Nothing.

"Shit! Shit! Shit!" She beat her hands against the wheel. She glanced up into the rear-view mirror at her two sleeping children. Mason and Bethany were her sweet little angels, barely fourteen months apart in age, at two and three, and thick as thieves. Mason had drool rolling down his chin, and Bethany snored softly. Their innocence made Susanna's heart ache. For them, everything was good now, and when they woke up, their world would be changed. She hated herself for it.

Susanna laid her head against the steering wheel and allowed herself to weep for the ancient car breaking down at the most inconvenient time, and for the whirlwind hell their lives had become over the last several months. She knew she should have been fair, for the kid's sake, and not taken off like that. But it was hard. When she thought about her husband, the person she loved and trusted most in the world in their bed with his secretary, her heart ached so badly she feared it would never recover.

She could kill him. God knew she could. That wouldn't solve anything though. Like it or not, rough as it may be, she was as responsible for the mess she was in. She'd made one mistake after another. Her babies, however, were not mistakes. She had to do what was best for them no matter what.

That started with collecting her nerves. She needed to pop the hood and find out what was wrong with this damn car.

"It's okay. It's okay," she whispered out loud, for no other reason but to comfort herself.

She straightened her spine, wiped the tears away, then turned to her children again. Sleeping like rocks. It was no wonder, really. They'd been through the ringer recently, and she knew they didn't understand what was happening. She felt horrible about that. She'd never meant to fight in front of the kids, and she knew they picked up on more than she wanted. She would have to find a way to make it up to them and explain that Mommy and Daddy wouldn't be living together anymore. She would never want them to hate David, no matter what happened between them. She needed to cool her head before she could make fair decisions, though. She glanced out the window at the dark night that ran on for endless miles like a black hole waiting to swallow up any sliver of light.

Susanna switched on the light and rummaged in her purse to find a hair tie to pull her long red hair away from her face. With her hair pulled she stared into the rearview mirror. Her eyes were bloodshot and puffy from crying, and her skin was covered in angry splotches of red. She'd cried the whole trip and was on the verge of starting again.

She popped the hood and walked around to the trunk and rummaged through the bags she'd packed last minute in search of a flashlight. She shivered against the biting cold wind that blew harder than before and ran her hands up her arms. She scolded herself silently as she searched. She made rash decisions when she was upset. It was a problem she'd been working on. She leaned against the back of the car, trying to shield herself from the cold, then glanced at the rear window where the slightest hint of ice crystals were beginning to form, and she feared the temperature would drop further. This could be bad. She rolled her eyes and gave herself a mental slap as she realized there were only shorts, skirts, and short sleeved shirts in her bag. At least she'd dressed the kids more sensibly. She continued to dig in the bags, found the flashlight, then saw a lightweight sweater wedged towards the back of the trunk that she'd forgotten about.

Susanna went around to the front of the car and checked what she knew. The oil was fine. There weren't any leaks that she could see, but then again, it was a little after two o'clock in the morning, and she didn't *really* know what she was doing. David took care of the cars. Not well it seemed. She sighed and shook her head. This car was older than dirt. She'd begged David to get a new one more times than she could count, but he always said it was a waste of money when the cars they had would do perfectly fine if they were kept up. One more thing she had to thank him for.

Susanna slammed the hood shut, sat down on it, and rubbed her knuckles against her tired eyes. She needed to think. She was in quite a predicament, and she was scared. How did she let this happen? Mallory, her sister, wasn't expecting her. She didn't even know where she was. How could she have been so stupid as to not stop at a motel when the kids started fussing? Before she was so tired that she wasn't paying attention to where she was going? Here she was with two toddlers in the middle of the night and had somehow managed to get off the highway. Should she wake the kids and try to walk an unforeseeable distance with them cranky and fighting every step of the way in this biting cold? Should she try to go for help herself while they were sound asleep? Or should she get back in the car, wait until morning and pray somebody came along? She shook her head at the thought and mentally slapped herself for even thinking of leaving.

She needed a phone, and she didn't know how long a walk it would be to find one. She knew the kids wouldn't want to walk. She wouldn't be able to carry them both for too long. Why couldn't she remember anything David was always saying about cars?

She closed her eyes. When she opened them back up there was a dim light off in the distance. She rubbed her eyes, but the light grew closer. When she heard the hum of an approaching engine, her heart soared.

Ignoring everything she'd been taught since birth she ran out directly in the middle of the road. She waved her arms and yelled as loud as she could, "Hey! Please stop!"

The old, red truck came to a stop next to her and the window rolled down. A middle-aged gentleman in a baseball cap stared out his window at her.

"Thank God!" Susanna exclaimed, put her hand to her chest, and leaned against the door of the pickup truck.

"Having some trouble, ma'am?" the man asked.

"Yes. It died on me. I'm passing through and had to exit the highway early. I got lost. I didn't know what to do."

"Well, let me see what I can do," the man said. He pulled his truck to the side of the road, in front of Susanna's car, and killed his headlights before stepping out.

He was dressed in dark clothing and the cap shadowed most of his face in the minimal lighting, but Susanna could see that he was tall and slightly on the pudgy side.

He approached her car and stood in front of it. "Pop the hood," he said with a deep gruff voice and not so much as a hint of genuine hospitality. Still, Susanna wasn't about to look a gift horse in the mouth. Not now. She popped the hood for him.

"Got a flashlight?" he asked her, then turned his head and spit chewing tobacco at his heels.

Disgusted at the habit, Susanna forced herself to hold her tongue and not lecture this stranger about the dangers of tobacco. "Yes, right here," she walked back up to him.

"Good. You hold it for me right here," he positioned the flashlight in her hands just so. "Steady. I'll be right back."

He walked back to his truck and rummaged in a toolbox, pulling out various tools he would need before coming back over. He worked soundlessly under the hood.

"I'm kind of clueless when it comes to cars," Susanna said nervously, trying to break the tense silence. "My husband always handles the cars."

"Does your husband always allow you to drive off in the middle of the night in an inferior vehicle?" he asked stiffly, without turning his head toward her.

Stunned, she stepped back. "Well, no. To tell you the truth we recently separated and that's why I'm on the road. Headed home. Boston was more his scene."

"Home to where?" he asked.

Finally, this man was engaging in conversation. It should be less awkward now.

"Georgia. Haven't been south in so long."

"Still got quite a way to go. You got kin there?"

"My sister is there. Still, it's where I grew up and is the only real home I've ever known. I'm sorry, where are my manners? Here you are working on my car, and I haven't properly introduced myself. I'm Susanna Patterson."

He hesitated a moment, then flicked his eyes toward her. "Pete Landers," he nodded at her. "You know, you should have stopped at a motel before you got off the highway. You're in the middle of no man's land. If I hadn't come along, you could have been in real hot water. There's nothing for quite a spell."

Susanna's stomach suddenly tightened and the chill in her spine returned, unrelenting and deep into the bone. She found herself wishing he would hurry up. "Well, as I said, I got off the highway by accident."

"Women have no business running around in the middle of the night by themselves in run-down cars."

Fury bubbled up inside of her, and her blood shot straight to her face and ears until she was certain they were beet red. "Now look here," she said, "I appreciate you helping me, which I understand full well you don't have to do, but that does not give you the right to insult me."

"I mean no offense, ma'am. I do apologize. I'm opinionated and I talk straight. Please don't take what I said as an insult."

They both heard the car door opening and closing. "Mama?" came the tiny, tired voice of little Bethany as she came around the front of the car. Clutching her favorite stuffed dog with one tiny hand and rubbing her eyes with the other, she stared up at her mother.

Pete Landers narrowed his eyes, and Susanna didn't know why, but she had an instant flash of panic. Bethany had been able to unclip her car seat for a couple of months now. She was an extremely observant child and could figure out things by watching people around her.

"You have a child with you?" he asked with that gruff voice of his.

"Two," she answered quietly, trying to keep her hands from shaking.

"Mama, I gotta pee," Bethany announced grumpily, placing her free hand on her hip and scowling up at her mother.

"It's alright. I got it. You go take care of her," Pete said, taking the flashlight from her.

Susanna turned, scooped up Bethany and walked behind the car with her, trying to still her nerves. She wished she had the flashlight for reasons she couldn't explain. The man's gruff nature made her uneasy, and she could almost feel the fury rolling off him like fire. She set the child down on the ground. "You'll have to go here, baby."

"Mama! Not the potty!" Bethany insisted.

"I know, baby, but you can't have a potty right now. We broke down."

"Broke down?" Bethany asked, cocking her tiny head to one side.

"It means the car stopped working. There isn't a potty for a long way, so you'll have to go here."

"Car sick!" Bethany exclaimed as she obeyed her mother and started to pee.

"Yes, exactly," Susanna said as she rummaged in the trunk and found a towel to clean her daughter up with. She could no longer hear the clank of tools, but she also hadn't heard the truck pull away. She wasn't sure which worried her more. Was the man listening to them?

Bethany shivered while Susanna cleaned her up. "I'm cold, Mama."

"I know, baby." Susanna pulled Bethany's pants back up, then pulled a heavier coat from the princess bag in the trunk. She put the coat on her daughter, zipping her up to the neck. She was annoyed at herself for not packing gloves. "Keep your hands in your pockets."

She carried Bethany back around to the rear driver-side door and opened it. The little girl cried grumpily as Susanna put her back in her seat. "I know, baby, but you need to stay in the car. We don't want you to get hit by a car, do we?"

"No," Bethany cried.

"It's okay. When the car is fixed, we'll stop somewhere for the night. I promise."

She walked back around to the front of the car and saw Pete had stopped working. He stood there, listening. "Cute kid."

"Yeah, they both are. But they're sick of the road."

"I imagine so," he said. There was a long awkward pause. "You can go ahead and try the engine now."

Susanna got in the driver's side of the car and tried the ignition. It kicked to life immediately. She exclaimed in joy. "Thank you! Thank you!" She rolled down the window as Pete approached and felt some of her fear ebbing away. "I don't know how to thank you."

"Well, it's my pleasure. Couldn't leave a young pretty thing like you stranded out here this time of night."

"Do you think it's safe to get back on the highway?"

"Probably not. This isn't a permanent fix. It's a bandage of sorts. Your best bet is to go to Jimmy Alderman's and trade it in. But of course, he's closed until eight o'clock tomorrow morning."

"I don't want to keep the kids in the car that long. I think I better get back on the highway and exit somewhere at a motel."

"All due respect, ma'am, I'm not convinced this car will make it that far without breaking down again. You're more than twenty miles off the highway. I think Alderman's is your safest bet. There's a little motel not terribly far from him."

She stopped a moment to consider and glanced at the little clock on her dash. It was now quarter past three. Holy hell. "Well, where is it?" she asked.

"'Bout a mile or so up the road you'll come to a fork. Follow it left. Then head straight for another two miles and you'll see Jimmy Alderman's shop on the left. A little way up the road there's a little motel. Dot in the road, really."

Susanna didn't like the idea of going further into the unknown, but she believed him that the highway was so far away.

She'd gotten lost a long time ago. There was the possibility she would get lost again or break down, and at least this way she knew exactly where she was going.

"Okay, I'll go and do that. Do I owe you anything? Where can I send you a little something once, we get home?"

"Oh, don't you even worry about that. I don't need a thing. You get yourself to safety, you hear?" He tapped the roof of the car twice.

"Well, alright," Susanna said. "Thank you again. Goodbye." She rolled up the window and waved again before pulling away. She was grateful for the help, naturally, but she was more than a little relieved to be leaving.

She followed his directions. Came to the fork in the road, right where he said it would be and took the left. She followed it down for another two miles and saw the auto shop closed, and in stark lighting. She knew the motel was nearby. Thank God.

Susanna was overjoyed about the blinking light right outside the office door. Civilization. Never would she take it for granted again. She glanced into the back seat. Both kids were sleeping once again. She decided not to wake them yet, and parked right outside the office so she could see them through the window, before going in to register.

The office was dimly lit, but had a homey feel to it with vases of flowers sitting around and scented candles lit. She rang the bell that sat on the counter. A door behind the counter opened and slightly plump, middle-aged woman with a name badge that read, "Sherry," greeted her warmly.

"Well, hello! Welcome to the Seaside Motel. Haven't seen you around here before."

"Oh, I'm passing through. I got off the highway by mistake and had some car trouble. I figure I need to give myself and my kids a break."

"Oh," the woman laughed and smiled. "I understand completely. Well, I'll need to get you to sign," she said, turning the register to her. "Are you just going to be with us the one night?"

"Hopefully. Planning on trading my car in at Jimmy Alderman's in the morning."

"Oh, I see," Sherry said, taking the credit card Susanna offered. She processed the payment and slid the card back across the counter towards her along with a room key. "I put you in room one. Right here next to the office so you don't have to take your little ones so far."

"Thank you, that's thoughtful," Susanna said. She thanked Sherry again, then went to open her room, hauling the sleeping kids inside one at a time. She placed them fully clothed in one bed together. She would take the other for herself for once. She brought in one of the bags from the trunk and debated whether to take a shower before hitting the sack. She surveyed the room and fought to stifle a groan. The room left a lot to be desired. It was spacious enough, with its two queen size beds, full sized dresser, and table and chairs that sat outside the bathroom. There was still an emptiness. It was as if years of neglect had riddled the place with sadness. While the room was well dusted, the air was hot and stuffy. Did it never get any air?

Susanna quietly went to the adjacent bathroom and left the door slightly ajar as she went in and took a quick ten-minute shower with the worst water pressure before finally slipping into the bed with its hard mattress that felt like heaven anyway and slipped into dreamland.

She dreamed of dark highways and baseball caps. She heard her children screaming and the sound of chewing tobacco hitting the earth, hitting her shoes. She heard a somewhat mocking tone in a gruff voice and heaviness engulfed her. She heard voices in her head and felt rough hands on her. It was all too real.

Eventually, as she tried to pull herself out of the nightmare, she realized she was no longer sleeping. There was someone in the darkness. Someone in the room with her. With her babies.

"Get the hell out!" she tried to scream and shoot to her feet, only to realize she'd been bound and gagged. She saw a figure moving through the darkness. A newly familiar figure. The figure of a tall pudgy man who wore a baseball cap. A horrible stench filled the room. Chewing tobacco.

"Oh God!" she thought to herself. What was she going to do? She'd been right to fear him before. And now she was helplessly bound and couldn't reach her babies. How was she so stupid as to go exactly to where a stranger had said? Of course he wanted her to come here! Come here so he could do God knew what to her and her children. Why the hell had she not gotten back on the highway?

"Think, Susanna, think!" she thought to herself. She tried to work the ropes that bound her hands behind her back and loosen them a bit, but they were tight and cut deep into her flesh. She let out a little involuntary whimper.

"No need trying to untie those ropes," he said with his gruff voice at last and clicked on the lamp. It was the man from the road, as she thought it would be. He stood in the dim light, his baseball cap still shielding his face. He wore gloves and wiped down the surfaces of the bedside table. There was no telling what he'd wiped clean. "You'll never get loose. Don't waste your energy."

She flicked her eyes over to the opposite bed, and her eyes went wide with shock. Her children were gone. He followed the direction of her gaze, then reached over to remove her gag.

She screamed with all her might. He chuckled and shook his head. "Scream all you want. There's nobody to hear."

"There's the receptionist," Susanna said with as much fire as she could muster in her voice. "Right next door in the office. She must have heard me. She probably already called the police. So, you should give me back my children and get out of here if you know what's good for you."

"Oh, the receptionist has already been taken care of," he said calmly and sat down on the opposite bed, the one her children were in when she'd fallen asleep. "And you can stop playing the act of concerned Mommy."

"What are you talking about?"

He sneered and gave a cold laugh so full of menace that it sent shivers down her spine. "I despise little bitches like you. You think the world and everybody in it owes you something. Owes you the world. Just because you're young and beautiful and show off your body you can get anything you please."

"That's not true at all," she said. Her voice quavered.

"Don't lie to me. You flag me down in the dead of night and expect me to fix your piece of shit car. I was taught to never leave a lady stranded so I stopped anyway out of the goodness of my heart. But you..." Anger rose in his voice, and he rose from the bed, pacing the room.

"What kind of a person, what kind of *mother,* takes their children away from their father and drives around willy nilly with no regard for their feelings or safety in the middle of nowhere? Who has their children out in this kind of cold, not even knowing where she is headed, forcing her child to piss behind a car on a dark stretch of road? I'll tell you who. Selfish, expectant little bitches like you. People like you don't deserve children! No regard for safety, doing everything on a whim, being thoughtless and stupid because you can!" He strode back over and slapped her face so hard, her teeth rattled in her skull and her head rocked to the side. She immediately tasted blood. "You deserve everything that happens. You *asked* for it!"

She did not cry out loud, but tears flowed freely down her face. "What did you do with them?"

"I did them a favor. You put them in harm's way more than once tonight. Would have continued to do so. Some mother. I put them out of their misery. You won't be hurting them anymore."

He suddenly leapt forward and grabbed her, threw her over his shoulder, and carried her out the door. She screamed. She tried to kick and hit him, but with the ropes tightly binding her, she wiggled wildly over his shoulder.

He threw her into the trunk of her own car. She knew it by Bethany's princess bag resting next to her head. He slammed the trunk door closed, muffling her screams and everything went dark.

Stacey-2022

Stacey Branch marched into the women's room of the newspaper office and splashed some water on her face before staring into the mirror. There were dark circles under her eyes, giving away the long hours she'd been working, and making her appear much older than her twenty-seven years.

She'd been on a mission for a while now in the world of investigative reporting to move up the ladder. She was a hell of a reporter, never stopping until she got to the bottom of her story. Unfortunately, the scandals of Lademan County were few and far between, and there was only so far she could go.

She dug a hair elastic out of her purse and pulled her long, blonde hair back into a messy bun before proceeding to the employee's lounge to make herself her umpteenth cup of coffee.

"You're still here?" Elinor Smith glanced up from her own cup of coffee and the trashy romance novel she was reading that proudly bore the chest of a muscular man.

"Burning the midnight oil at both ends," Stacey laughed, and brought her coffee over to sit across from her friend. "I'm trying to finish that report on Grandma's so it can go to press in the morning."

"Honey, it's a chef that doesn't wash his hands," Elinor gave her a friendly nudge. "It's not worth killing yourself over."

"But it's the biggest story I've had in months," she sighed. "Besides, it's a little more than that. He sexually harasses the wait staff."

"Well, that makes it a little juicier," Elinor winked at her and squeezed her hand. "But I still think you ought to go home. You're not on deadline and the pervert with crusty hands can wait an extra day."

Stacey snorted out a nose full of coffee and laughed hysterically. "Don't do that to me, Ellie! It burns!"

"Sorry," her friend giggled and handed Stacey a napkin to wipe the coffee from her nose.

"I probably shouldn't go back right now. It's so late."

"You still with your folks?"

Stacey nodded. Her exhaustion wasn't only related to her work. She'd temporarily moved in with her parents last month after her mother had a small stroke. They refused to hire a nurse, but her mother needed more care than her father could provide. Her mother was improving, but Stacey still wasn't comfortable moving back to her apartment. Her parents' 'simple' way of living didn't leave her confident they'd be okay.

They insisted on living off the land, and the old generator in the shed was the only thing in the way of modern conveniences. No running water, no electricity. They were totally off the grid, and it led to plenty of drama when Stacey was a kid. When she'd moved in to help, she'd pleaded for three days straight to have a flashlight. They wanted her to use oil lamps to get around like they did, but those things had always made her nervous.

"Honey," Elinor said gently. "You moved in to help your mama, but you can't do that if you're never home. It's not like they can call you if something's wrong."

Stacey sighed loudly and tightly squeezed her friend's hand. "You're right. As always. Damn you to hell, Ellie."

Elinor grinned. "You know you love me."

Stacey pulled out her cell phone and checked that it had a healthy charge before rising to her feet. "Promise you'll let me know if something happens?"

"Don't I always?" Elinor stuck out her pinky finger, prompting another bout of giggles from Stacey.

Fifteen minutes later, Stacey traveled down Route 6 and couldn't stop the shivers that ran down her spine. It didn't matter how long she lived here, this feeling of doom always hit her when she traveled down this road, especially at night. There was nothing for miles, and no lights. But the small town of DeSoto only had this one road running through it, and it was the only way to get to her parents' farmhouse.

Almost on cue, the car sputtered before finally dying out.

"What?" she muttered before trying the ignition again. Nothing happened. "Shit!" She pounded the steering wheel and pulled out her phone.

Thankful to see she had bars, she called her brother, Gavin.

"Stace?" Gavin's voice was groggy with sleep, but he sounded concerned.

"Hello, sweet brother of mine. I have a problem."

"Stacey, it's almost three in the morning. Are you okay?"

"I'm fine, but I have a bone to pick with you. Didn't you tell me when you sold me this car it ran like a cat, and I couldn't find anything more reliable? Well, I've had it less than a week and it broke down."

"What? That's not possible. I double checked everything on it myself." Stacey heard creaking and rustling as he got out of bed. "Where are you? I'll come get you."

"On Route 6 headed back to Mom and Dad's."

"You're a pain in my ass, Blondie. I'll take you home, but I'm going to have to sit there and listen to more lectures."

"You brought it on yourself this time."

"Okay, okay. Give me fifteen."

He hung up the phone, and Stacey leaned back in her seat to wait. She didn't have the car radio, she didn't want to listen to a playlist on her phone and drain the battery, and it was way too dark to read.

This damn stretch of road grew even more intimidating as the minutes stretched by. She didn't know if it was because of the late hour or because she had nothing to do, but Stacey's gut clenched in an unnatural way. Everything in her was telling her to run, but she didn't understand why.

Off in the distance, she thought she saw something moving in the shadows. An animal? No. She didn't think so. She turned on high beams to see another car about twenty feet ahead of her. And the outline of a pair of legs moving behind it.

Stacey got out of the car and walked ahead, making sure to stay in the line of her car's headlights. As she approached, the temperature dropped, and she crossed her arms tightly across her chest. A woman knelt behind the old car with a child, shielding her from something with her body.

"Excuse me!" Stacey called out. "Are you alright?"

The woman didn't answer her and reached into the trunk and dug through the contents. The child clumsily pulled her pants up.

"My brother is on his way if you need help," Stacey called out to her again, her heart rate rising. "He's a mechanic."

The woman ignored her, and Stacey opened her mouth to say something else, but she was cut off by the tooting of a horn. She turned back to see Gavin pulling up alongside her car.

"That's him," she breathed in relief. "I'll bring him right over."

She jogged back to the car, and as she pulled even with the front bumper, the ignition spurted to life.

Gavin leaned out the driver's side door, his brow furrowed with confusion. "Are you trying to piss me off?"

"What are you talking about?"

"There's nothing wrong with this car, Stacey."

"It died on me mid-drive!" she insisted. "I couldn't get the engine to turn over."

"Funny how I had no issues," he grumbled and slammed the door shut.

"Well, it's not all lost. There's a woman broken down up the road, so you'll still get to help someone."

Gavin stared pointedly over her shoulder before rolling his eyes. "Go home and get some sleep, Stace. You're making me worry about you."

He walked toward his own car, and Stacey grabbed his arm as he passed in front of her.

She turned to call out to the woman but was astonished to see nothing but empty road. "What?" her voice cracked, and she squinted, willing the woman and her child to reappear.

"I really am worried about you, Stacey."

Stacey turned to peer into her brother's eyes and saw a softness that hadn't been there a moment ago. "There was a woman up there, I swear."

"How long have you been at work?"

Stacey sputtered in aggravation and threw up her arms. "Jesus, that's not relevant."

"How long?"

"Three days."

"You're telling me you haven't slept in three days?"

"No, I've slept. I haven't come home."

"So, cat naps then?"

"Don't make it sound like that."

Gavin slumped against the car. "Angie wants you to come for dinner soon."

"That's what you're thinking of right now?"

"Call it a peace offering," he gave her a crooked grin. "Besides, she's been on my ass for days about it."

"I'll call her when I wake up." Stacey hugged him and laid a sloppy kiss on his cheek.

"For the love of God," he lovingly pushed her away and wiped his cheek.

She laughed. "I'm sorry you came out here for nothing. I don't know what's going on now, but it really did stop."

"Don't worry about it. I probably wouldn't have been able to see your dorky ass for another week if I didn't come."

She went in for another kiss, and he backed away in mock terror, warding her off with his hands. "I believe you. Keep your spit in your mouth."

"Shithead," she laughed.

When Stacey pulled in front of the farmhouse twenty minutes later, she was still shaken from her experience on the road. As she stepped out of the car, her body relaxed. She'd always found the quiet of the farm calming. Late at night all she could hear was the hooting of owls and the chirping of crickets. Enough noise to keep from being creepy, but not so much that it was disturbing. No loud horns at 3 a.m. No flashing lights in her bedroom window. It was nice.

Stacey tiptoed through the kitchen door and grabbed her flashlight from a drawer, using it to guide her to the stairs and up to her bedroom.

She didn't even bother changing into pajamas before collapsing in the bed. When she awoke the next morning, her mind automatically flew to her strange experience on the road. She *had* seen that woman and her child. She was sure of it. But where did they go? Even stranger was her car breaking down when nothing was wrong with it. She'd looked like an idiot in front of Gavin.

She quickly dressed and went downstairs where she found her parents in the kitchen. She smiled and gave her mama a kiss on the cheek.

Alice Branch was short in stature and slightly plump. Her face always carried a smile, and she looked for the best in every situation. She was Stacey's rock and the only reason she and Gavin had any independence at all. She'd fought for them to be allowed to go to public school.

"Look who finally came home," Alice smiled and then studied her daughter's face. "You're working too hard, baby. At that newspaper office at all hours."

"I'm okay, Mama," Stacey assured her before turning to her father who sat at the kitchen table and bending down to give him a peck on the cheek. "Morning, Daddy."

He stared at her, irritation evident on his face. "You mean, afternoon. It's after one. We're getting ready to have lunch, not breakfast."

Had she really slept that long? Stacey glanced at the wall clock and was astonished to see her father was right. It was a quarter after one.

He glared at her, making her blush. "It was a long night. I didn't get in until late."

"Are you hungry? I can make you a sandwich," Alice interjected.

"No, I'm okay. You sit down and eat. I moved in here to take care of you," Stacey said as she pointed toward the vacant seat opposite her father.

"Lot of good that does when you're never here."

He might as well have slapped her. She'd often felt guilty when she had to go to work, but it was a whole other monster to basically be told she was a bad daughter.

"Daddy, I—" she whispered, unable to figure out what to say to him.

"I worry about your mother constantly," he went on. "Do you have any idea how exhausting it is to take care of the whole farm when I keep running back inside to make sure she's okay? I thought I was going to get some help around here."

"Daddy, I have to work too."

He sneered. "Your mother should come first. Family always comes first, Stacey. Jobs come and go. Besides, that job is no good for you anyway. Your brother dropped by this morning. Told us about your little hallucination on the road."

"Gavin was here?" That surprised her. Gavin hardly ever came to the farmhouse. He had a volatile relationship with their parents, especially their father. Paul could be overly controlling, not even allowing them to have friends over as children, except for her best friend Beth. It had been that way as long as she could remember. Gavin signed a lease in the next town over the moment he'd turned eighteen and had maybe been back a total of twelve times since then.

"He was worried about you," Alice answered.

"He shouldn't be. The car broke down. It must have been a glitch in the engine or something. It was fine when he got to me, so he was a little irritated."

"He said you saw something that wasn't there."

Stacey's heart thundered in her chest, but she kept her voice even as she answered. "I thought I saw another car. It was several feet ahead. Probably a trick of the light. You know how distorted shadows can be out there."

Her father snorted. "Nonetheless, if you're seeing things, I think it's about time you stay home. Clearly, this job is too taxing."

"Daddy, this has been my dream as long as I can remember."

"Dreams. That's the problem. You're a little too old to be so focused on dreams. It's time you focus on reality. We need you here, and your body is telling you that's where you belong."

"Oh, leave her alone, Paul," Alice said sweetly. "I am worried about you, dear. You should at least not be gone for days at a time. A person needs sleep. I mean, seeing things while driving—"

Stacey's irritation began to gnaw at her, and she found herself wanting to go right back to the office. Now. "It was a shadow. That's all. Can we not make such a big deal about it, please?"

Her father was about to say something but was cut off by the sound of Stacey's cell phone ringing.

"For goodness' sake, Stacey," Alice admonished. "Do you have to have that thing in the house?"

"Sorry," Stacey apologized and headed toward the back door. "It's my boss."

Once she'd closed the door behind her, she answered the phone and Elinor's excited voice babbled immediately. Okay, she'd lied about it being her boss. She'd needed out of the conversation.

"Stacey, I've got news for you, girl!"

"What is it? You sound like you're going to a theme park for the first time."

"I'm excited for you, chick. The biggest thing to happen to these parts in years and you get to cover it! I suggested you to Mike. But he agreed."

"The biggest thing, what?" Stacey asked in confusion. "Maybe we should back up a little bit."

"Girl, a car was pulled out of the lake behind the Seaside Hotel this morning. It's apparently been there awhile. Mike wants you out there pronto. It's going to be tricky since the police from Logan's Ridge are handling it. DeSoto doesn't have its own police force anymore, you know."

"You're sure he said me?"

"Absolutely, now hurry up and get out there before one of the other newspapers gets the scoop first!"

Stacey excitedly ran back inside the house to grab her car keys.

CHAPTER THREE

Stacey was baffled when she pulled up on the road in front of the Seaside Motel. The place bustled with more activity than she could ever remember seeing. News vans and police cruisers were all over the street. She got out of her car and walked around the side of the motel.

Crime scene tape was wrapped around trees, not letting her get close to the action. She craned her neck to see around the heads of the police before finally spotting the car.

It sat right at the edge of the lake, lopsided. It was a heavily rusted old Honda. The trunk hung open like a wide mouth, but she was unable to see what was inside.

Stacey took a moment to scan the grounds and noted there were no tire treads or damage to any of the surrounding trees. That, with the condition of the car, was enough to tell her whatever happened wasn't any time recent.

She caught the eye of one of the officers on the scene. Easton Gates was a tall, lanky man with a chiseled jaw, chestnut hair, and bright blue eyes. He was devilishly handsome, and she instantly hated he was working on it. She shouldn't have been surprised.

They'd been on exactly one date prior, and it was abundantly clear they were a train wreck. They'd sat in silence most of the time, and when they did speak, they took turns offending each other. Neither had reached out to the other since, and she'd been thankful she never needed to come up with a half-baked excuse not to go out again.

Easton grinned, said something to the person he'd been talking to, and walked toward her.

"Shit. Why is he coming over here?" Desperately, Stacey searched for a place to hide but there was nowhere to go.

"Hey, Stace," Easton said as he pulled even with her.

His casual use of the nickname annoyed her. Stace was for friends and family, not disastrous ex-dates. Still, it could help to be on good terms with someone on the inside.

"Hey," she shot him the fakest smile she could manage. "Big day, huh?"

"You know I can't fraternize with the press." His voice wasn't admonishing. He taunted her, still giving her that irritating grin.

She gritted her teeth. "I didn't ask for any specific information. All I said is it's a big day. I can't remember the last time something happened in DeSoto."

"It's been a while," he agreed. "Since something happened here and since we went out."

"Easton," she sighed. "We have nothing in common."

"Not true. We both eat dinner. Let me take you to dinner."

She sighed. She would love to get him talking about the car, but she didn't want to upset her parents by coming home late again.

"I told Mom and Dad I'd have dinner with them. But I'll give you lunch at Viola's."

"Alright. It'll be a few more minutes before I finish up here. Do you mind waiting?"

"Not at all."

~

Stacey sat in her car outside Viola's café until Easton pulled up in his police cruiser and they walked in together.

"I'll be right with you!" Miss Viola called over to them. "Sit anywhere you want!"

They selected a table for two next to the window and sat before Easton started a conversation.

"I was real sorry to hear about your mama," he said apologetically.

"Thanks. She's doing a lot better. A little weak but she's getting around more."

"I guess you're still staying there."

"How did you know about that?"

He cocked his head to the side. "Really?"

Stacey immediately realized he was right. Their mothers were friends. Alice and Teresa met in a church group a few years before. The church was three towns over, and they considered it fate they both lived in Logan's Ridge. It had always been mystifying to Stacey. Her parents didn't have friends, since they stayed holed up in the farmhouse like they did. But she'd taken to Teresa relatively fast. The date they'd gone out on had been at their mothers' insistence.

"Of course, where's my head?" she nodded. "Yeah, I'm still there. Mom's doing a lot better. Until I mention moving home. Then she'll start feeling bad again or end up spending the day in bed. Or Dad will start in about how much work he has to do, and he can't leave her alone. He doesn't even want me working right now."

"You know I like your folks, Stace," he carefully prodded. "But are you sure they aren't taking advantage of the situation to get you to do what they want?"

The statement annoyed her, but she couldn't deny it. The thought passed through her mind more than once. Neither she nor Gavin had been exactly what they'd wanted, and it led to tense teenage years. Things were worse with Gavin, but she'd gotten her fair share of the fight too.

"I mean it wasn't just you," Easton prodded further. "They freaked out when your brother moved instead of staying and working on the farm, right?"

Damn him and his inside knowledge. She didn't realize he would know this much. Her parents were private people. Having a friend was one thing. Divulging such things was another. Her mother must have been confident she was in the right to say anything to Teresa.

She was cut off by Viola approaching their table and taking their orders. The process only bought her a couple of minutes, but at least she was able to collect her thoughts.

"They weren't happy with Gavin, that's true," she admitted. "Our family is tight knit. It's only us left. They don't want to die alone."

Easton was skeptical but nodded for her to continue.

"The way Gavin and I handled things was different. He took off the second he turned eighteen and hardly ever visits. When he does, there's always a fight. They feel like he abandoned them. With me, I always stayed present. Even before Mom's stroke, I'd go for dinner with them a couple of times a week. I dropped in all the time. Brought groceries. Sure, they'd like me to be closer, but I'm still very much there for them."

"So, they're not pushing you to stay?"

"Well, Dad is. Kind of. He's always saying he can't do much on the farm because he's constantly having to go check on her. That's kind of the reason I came back anyway. But I'm not able to do it full time. He's made a few comments about how if I'm not there to take the pressure off him, it's pointless that I moved back at all."

Easton nodded and gave her a half smile.

"I've been waiting for a big story. Hoping if I get something big enough, I'll be able to cut back my hours and be home more. I was disappointed to be out of the jurisdiction to those missing girl cases last year."

Easton cocked an eyebrow. "Are you saying you're glad there was a serial roaming around?"

"No!" she exclaimed. "Of course not. But it would have at least been something to write about besides an unhygienic, pervy chef."

"Grandma's?"

She shuddered, initiating a chuckle from Easton.

"But like today," she continued, "I doubt whatever happened with that car is good, but it's bound to be the story I need to get me out of my slump."

Easton's expression suddenly turned stony. "Stacey, as much as I like you, you're still a member of the press. I can't tell you about the case."

"I don't need you to," she said calmly. "I have eyes of my own. The ground was undisturbed. There weren't any marks on the trees. The car was rusted all to hell. This wasn't a recent wreck."

He sighed and peered out the window for a moment before turning back to her. "Alright, look. This didn't come from me, but I guess there's no harm in telling you. Chief's going to be holding a press conference soon."

"I won't put anything in print until then."

He nodded. "We checked the VIN and registration. The car is tied to a cold case."

Her eyes went wide in surprise. "I didn't know DeSoto had any cold cases."

"That's the thing," he said, lowering his voice and leaning forward slightly. "The people that went missing were from Boston. They were traced as far as DeSoto before they disappeared."

"People?"

"A woman and her two children."

"Who was it?"

The conspiratorial grin was back. "Now, you know I can't tell you that. Not before the press conference."

She shrugged. She could find out easily enough. His phone buzzed and he checked it.

"Shit. I'm so sorry. It's the chief. I have to go. I'll take a rain check, okay?"

She nodded but he made his way toward the door before she could respond. It was less than a minute before Viola came back to the table with their plates.

"Where's Mr. Gates?"

"Duty calls." Stacey smiled. "His chief called him. I'm guessing he had to go back to The Seaside Hotel. I'm not sure if you know, but there's a lot going on down there this morning."

"I heard," Viola nodded and gazed out the window in the direction of the hotel. "The car. I wonder if it has to do with that night."

Stacey narrowed her eyes. "What do you mean? What night?"

"Oh, that's right. You didn't live here then," Viola looked down at her and smiled. "There was one night back before the hotel closed that I saw a light in the window. See, the hotel was still open, but they weren't doing well. Not a lot of business. No one believed me. Even after that detective came sniffing around. Tony Bradford said he saw something that night too, but they barely investigated. Asked a few questions, then went back to where they came from. We never heard anything about it again." She shook her head.

"Such a shame. I've often wondered about that poor woman. Disappearing without a trace like that and no one seems to care."

"When did this happen?"

"It was 1996. There hasn't been a day since I haven't thought about it."

Stacey's stomach clenched. Easton said it was a cold case, but she hadn't expected it to be that cold. This case would be even bigger than she thought.

CHAPTER FOUR

Twenty minutes later, Stacey pulled up in front of the hut of Tony Bradford. Tony was the town hermit.

From her perspective outside, the hut was like a tiny storage shed, but it was well kept. She strolled up to the door and knocked.

Tony answered. His face was scruffy from facial hair and his hair was long and tussled. Dark shadows riddled his eyes which were narrowed on her. "Yes?"

"Mr. Bradford? I'm Stacey Branch." She extended her hand for him to shake, but he didn't take it. Instead, he glanced down at her hand as if it were a snake readying for a strike.

She pulled back her hand and smiled at him. "I'm investigating the car that was pulled out of the lake this morning. Down at The Seaside Hotel."

"You're a cop?"

"No," she vigorously shook her head. "I'm a reporter. From the Logan's Ridge newspaper office."

He narrowed his eyes at her for a moment and then stepped to the side to allow her inside.

The inside of the hut was one room. A counter, stove, and sink on one wall, a bathtub and toilet on another, with a curtain to separate them, and a tiny living space.

Tony gestured toward a small dining table for her to sit, and she followed his lead.

"I saw something was going on down there, but I didn't know what it was. I prefer to stay away from crowds."

Stacey nodded. She'd figured this about him. They'd never officially met. Any time she'd seen him before, he'd always been walking down the road alone.

"I'm not sure how I can help you."

"Well, I have it on good authority the car is linked to an incident from 1996."

Tony shifted in his chair and grew fascinated with a thread hanging from the torn knees in his jeans.

Stacey pressed on. "Do you know Miss Viola?"

"From the café?" His focus shifted to her. "I do. Real nice lady. She'll often set aside a meal for me and let me pick it up at the backdoor after closing."

"I love her so much," Stacey agreed. "I used to go to school with her granddaughter, and we'd have sleepovers and stuff. She's always been like a grandma to me."

"God love her."

"Absolutely. So, I talked to her today and she told me about a strange night in '96. She said she saw a light in one of the windows, but no one believed her. Only a few days later, there was an investigation about a missing woman. The car that was found this morning belongs to that same woman. Miss Viola mentioned you saw something that night as well, and I wonder what you saw."

Tony sighed before answering her in a gentle tone. "Miss, you seem nice, but there ain't no reason to talk about that night. No one believed me then. No one will believe me now. They never do."

"Give yourself a little credit," she said as gently as she could. "There's evidence now this woman was here. You could be taken more seriously. I promise I will listen to you. I won't print anything if you don't want me to. But it could help put the pieces together."

"It's going to sound crazy." He took a deep breath before launching into his story. "I walk when I'm anxious, I walk when I can't sleep. You get the idea. I couldn't sleep that night. So, I bundled up in a coat, grabbed my dog so he could get a nice walk and off we went."

"I walked down the side of Route 6 and I saw a car pulled over on the side. The headlights cut through the darkness and a woman sat on the hood crying. I was about to walk up to help her, but a truck drove up and she flagged it down. I figured she was in good hands and went back towards my house."

"I don't see why people didn't believe you about that."

"It was the next part that was basically ignored." He snorted, and his eyes flashed with anger. "I went out again about an hour so later. This time, I walked across from the motel. I was surprised to see a light in one of the windows. It happened so rarely. I looked in that direction when the commotion started."

His eyes focused on a point over her shoulder, almost as if he were transported to another time, and his lip quivered.

"The door to that room busted open and a man came out with a woman slung over his shoulder. He threw her into the trunk of the car sitting outside and drove off. It happened so quickly. I ran up to the office to tell the receptionist, Sherry, to call the police.

His voice cracked as he continued. "The door to the back room was open and a television was playing cartoons. A couple of kids were sitting there watching, exhausted."

Stacey's stomach clenched painfully. She hadn't mentioned the woman went missing with her children.

"Sherry stepped out of the back room and shut the door. I asked her who the kids were, and she said her sister's kids were visiting from out of state and then asked me what I needed. I told her what I'd seen, and she told me she didn't have any customers that night, so I had to be mistaken. I told her the light was still on in the room, and she snapped at me to not be a busybody. She didn't have any customers, and the housekeeper might have left the light on. I was surprised because Sherry was usually a joy to be around. She was such a genuinely sweet person that reaction surprised me. I went home, but I still felt off about what I saw."

Tears slowly slid down his cheeks. "When those detectives showed up in town and were nosing around the motel, I knew what it was about, and I went to tell them what I saw. The guy in charge listened, but it was clear he didn't believe a word I said. They never came to talk to me again, and the chatter around it died down after a couple of days. I never forgot though. I've always felt if I'd pushed Sherry harder, maybe someone could have found the guy. You said the car belongs to the missing woman?"

"That's what my source said," Stacey answered. She hesitated a moment before pulling out her phone to pull up the photos of the car she'd taken at the scene. "I know it was dark and you weren't close, but would you mind taking a look at this picture and telling me if you think it might have been the car you saw?"

He studied the photo, tightened his lips, and nodded. "That's definitely it."

"Was it the same car at the motel? Do you think it was the same woman you saw on the side of the road?"

"It's hard to say. It was so dark, and I was across the road. The only light was the one shining through the window of the room she was in and the light in the office. I didn't get a good look at the car but it's the only thing that makes sense. The motel would go weeks without anyone staying there. What are the odds someone would be there the same night there was a car broken down?"

"Do you think it was the person she waved down?"

"I doubt it. The reason I backed off and went home was because Marty Randall stopped to help her. I worked with him at Jimmy Alderman's. He was a decent mechanic, so I figured she was in good hands. Marty and I weren't crazy about each other, but he was good with cars."

"His truck wasn't at the motel?"

"Not that I saw."

"Do you know where he is now? How can I reach him?"

"Last I heard, he moved to California with Sherry a few weeks after that. I never heard anything about them after that. But no one ever tells me anything."

"With Sherry?" she asked, confused.

He nodded. "They were married."

"One last question. Do you remember which room you saw the light in?"

"I'll never forget. One. It was room one."

Chapter Five

"Hey there, lovelies!" Stacey kissed her mother's cheek after walking in the kitchen door.

Alice beamed as she moved a pot of mashed potatoes to the kitchen table. "Well, look who's here!"

"I told you I'd be home for dinner, didn't I?"

"Would have been nice if you'd been here to help your mother," Paul admonished from his spot at the table.

"I did," Stacey said through gritted teeth as she held up the bag in her hands. "I brought dessert. Blueberry pie. Your favorite, Daddy."

The room was lit from the various oil lamps sitting around, which gave it a spooky glow. The smell of the hearty meal was heavenly. Alice was always a great cook. Stacey loved to inhale her mother's meals.

When the women took their seats, they chattered among themselves.

"So, why did you tear out of here so fast this afternoon?" Alice asked.

"I got assigned to a big case. I had to go check it out."

Her father snorted. "Did someone get pink eye from the food at that Chinese restaurant again?"

Stacey bit back her sharp retort and instead answered evenly. "No, actually. A couple of fishermen found a car submerged in the lake this morning. Right behind The Seaside Motel."

Alice set down her fork and glanced up at her, concern evident in her eyes. "You mean there was a car accident?"

Stacey shook her head and took a sip of her water. "No. Not recently anyway. There was no disturbance at the site. Plus, Easton Gates told me the car was registered to a woman that went missing back in '96."

Alice continued to stare at her, slack jawed. "Around here?"

"That's what it looks like."

"Well," Paul said as he cut a slice of blueberry pie. "If that's true, it could get dangerous. You should leave it alone and let the police handle it."

"The police are handling it. I'm writing an article."

"As long as that's all it is."

After Stacey did the dinner dishes and helped her mother to bed, she made her way to a local coffee shop to take advantage of the free Wi-Fi. She ordered a biscuit and a juice to justify taking up a table and dove into her research.

Easton said the missing woman was from Boston, so she decided to start there. She searched for missing person cases for Boston 1996 and slowly narrowed the list down. She eliminated people that were too young, those who were alone, and solved cases until she was positive she'd found her girl.

She came across a video for an old newscast. She pulled her earbuds out of her bag so she wouldn't disturb the other patrons and hit play.

"In breaking news, it has been discovered wife of local banker, David Patterson, Susanna, has gone missing. The woman was

on a road trip to see her sister, along with her two small children. Once David and the sister spoke and it was discovered neither knew the whereabouts of the mother and children, the authorities were called.

Authorities tracked them to Virginia where the trail ran cold. If anyone has any information that can lead to the safe return of this family, please call the number on the screen."

Pictures of a smiling family flooded the screen with a 1-800 number stamped across the bottom of the screen.

This had to be her. How many mothers from Boston traveling with two kids went missing in 1996? She smiled inwardly at finally having a name and searched for it.

After searching for another hour, she was able to discover Susanna Patterson and her children were never found. Eventually the police stated they believed Susanna took off to start over. David Patterson publicly stated he did not believe that to be the case though he was granted a divorce by the courts a couple of years later.

Stacey sat back from her computer screen and chewed her lip. Nothing she found explicitly said Susanna was at the Seaside Motel, but she had to assume that to be the case. Her car was there, and two witnesses saw a random light in the window.

She dug out her cell phone and called Elinor. "Hey, chick. How would you like to go on an adventure?"

"This is crazy," Elinor said two hours later when they walked up to the dark motel.

"I understand if you want to go back," Stacey told her.

"Are you kidding?" Elinor laughed. "How often do we get the chance to do something like this around here?"

They'd decided to park a block away and walk the rest of the distance to lessen their chances of being seen. The motel may have been abandoned, but it was still private property.

They came to a stop outside the office, and Stacey reached her hand toward the knob. When it turned easily in her hand, she turned back toward Elinor, agape. "It's not even locked!"

They walked into the office and turned on the flashlights on their cell phones to search. The office was still in surprisingly good shape. There was no graffiti or litter, only dust. If they hadn't known better, it would've been easy to believe the office was closed for the night. There were still candles and magazines on end tables for customers. Room keys still hung from a pegboard behind the reception desk.

Stacey rounded the reception desk and examined the items behind it. There were ledgers, a safe hidden in a corner, and various office supplies in a drawer. She found the registration book on a shelf and blew a layer of dust off it. "I found the register!" she called out before plopping the book on the desk and beginning to scan the dates.

It appeared the motel was profitable. Multiple bookings at first and then gradually going down in 1993. Eventually, it tapered to one booking every few weeks. The last entry was clearly printed with the name Susanna Patterson. Bingo.

"She was the last customer the motel ever had," she told Elinor.

"Seriously?" the older woman came over to see. "That makes this even creepier."

"Tell me about it." Stacey ran her finger across the page to check the date. "According to this, she was only here a few hours, and she was reported missing two days later."

"You said the police did come here."

Stacey nodded. "They tracked her this far before her trail fizzled. A lot of the police reports were redacted so a lot of things are still confusing. I was able to see they eventually dropped the case, claiming she disappeared voluntarily, but not why they came to that conclusion."

"I'd say someone dropped the ball," Elinor said.

"I agree," Stacey nodded. "Let's see if we can find out how badly." She turned to the pegboard and seized the key for room one, slipping it in her pocket. "When we get done in here, we'll take a little peek in Susanna's room."

"Come check this out," Elinor called to her. She stood before a closet and knelt on the floor; her phone flashlight extended in front of her.

Stacey walked over to her and peered over her shoulder. There was a dark stain on the carpet at the bottom of the closet. "Is this blood?"

Stacey gently nudged Elinor out of the way. "One way to find out." She pulled a box cutter out of her bag and sliced the carpet.

"Stacey!" Elinor instinctively glanced over her shoulder as if concerned someone was going to walk in the door and bust them.

Stacey placed the square of carpet in an evidence baggie and slid it in her bag. "It's not like anyone's going to miss it."

She moved to the door behind the desk and opened it up. It appeared to be a smaller office. There was a desk along one wall with a small television on it. *"Well, that brings validity to Tony's story,"* she thought to herself.

There was a wall of shelves along the opposite wall, with various sized bins on them. The women peeked in the bins, not sure what they were looking for but knowing it would be obvious when they found it.

"Here. Lost and found!" Elinor exclaimed. There was one item in the bin. It was a carefully folded children's blanket printed with various fairy tale princesses. A piece of paper was pinned to the front. The note stated the blanket was found in the office the day after Susanna stayed there.

Stacey and Elinor exchanged glances and placed the blanket in the bag. They carefully scanned the two rooms again before moving onto room one.

It was a standard motel room, though outdated. Two queen-sized beds along one wall and a dresser with an old television on it. There was a small table and chairs outside the bathroom.

There was nothing obvious sitting out, but Stacey's intuition told her there was something there. She got on her hands and knees to examine every nook, cranny, and corner. She was mostly met with cobwebs until she got to the bed nearest the window. Wedged between the bedside table and the post for the bed was a small stuffed dog with a hole in the ear and a missing eye.

As soon as she held the dog in her hand, Stacey became overwhelmed with sorrow. She instinctively knew this belonged to one of Susanna's children, and it was well loved. She couldn't help but think this one wasn't going to have a happy ending.

"How did the police miss that?" Elinor asked with a hand to her mouth.

"How did they miss the stain in the closet?" Susanna whispered as she dug out an evidence bag. "They clearly did a piss-poor job investigating."

When she drove Elinor back to the newspaper office to get her car, Stacey saw the headlights of a car on the side of the road with a woman peering under the hood. She slammed on the brakes, causing Elinor to brace herself against the dashboard.

"What's wrong, chick?" Elinor asked.

"Look behind us. Do you see a car? Maybe a woman?"

Elinor did as she asked. "No one's there, hun."

Stacey flicked her eyes up to the rearview mirror and saw Elinor was right. Absolutely nothing there. She took a deep breath, nodded her head, and continued to drive.

CHAPTER SIX

"Theo! Theo!" Stacey banged her palm against the desk until it stung.

Theo Robins turned around, pulled the earbuds out of his ears, and smiled at her. They'd gone to high school together and had a somewhat unusual friendship.

"What's up, Stace?" he asked. His hair was unkempt as if he'd forgotten the purpose of a hairbrush, and his lab coat was splattered with a mystery substance she didn't want to know about.

"I'm glad you asked," she smiled. She plopped her bag up on the desk and pulled out the baggie with the carpet in it and the children's blanket. "You know that favor you owe me? I'm calling it in."

The year before, Theo's brother got into trouble with substances. The number of people that knew about his problem was extremely limited. One of the people that did know was a senior writer at the newspaper who planned on exposing him. Stacey hacked into her computer and erased her hard drive, which included pictures, making her unable to write the article. Theo thanked her immensely and said he'd be happy to help her on a big case in the future. She hadn't found anything big enough to require his help since.

"Finally got a big story, huh?" he grinned at her.

"Bigger than anyone realizes if I'm right," she pointed to each baggie in turn. "I believe this carpet has blood on it. I'd like to know if I'm right and possibly who it belongs to. I don't see anything wrong with the blanket, but it may have trace evidence on it. Can't hurt to check."

"You got it," he grabbed the bags from her. "I'm assuming this is off the books?"

"Absolutely."

"Where'd you get this stuff anyway?"

"I'm afraid that's classified."

He narrowed his eyes at her. "You broke into the motel?"

"How'd you know?"

"Come on. What else is going on in these parts? Besides, the police already have me checking a few things from the car. You know this won't be admissible, right?"

"Of course. But it may lead me to something that is."

"Alright, lady. So, where exactly was the stain?"

"A closet in the office."

"It could belong to anyone."

"It could," she agreed, "but my gut is telling me it doesn't and I'm usually right about these things."

"Okay. Well, I'll definitely be able to tell you if it's blood, but unless her DNA is already in the system, which is unlikely, I won't know if it's hers. It would help to have something to test it against."

Stacey nodded. "I'm working on it. Thanks for your help, Theo."

Disappearance on Route 6

"Stacey!" As soon as the door to Gavin's apartment opened, Stacey found herself enveloped in the biggest hug. "Hello, stranger!"

Angie smiled and pulled her into the apartment. She was Gavin's wife of two years, and they'd dated an additional five years prior to that. She was literally the sweetest person Stacey knew. Their parents hated her.

"Oh, look. It's the dork." Gavin winked at her from the dining room, where he was setting the table.

"Haha, very funny," she walked over to him and punched him in the shoulder where he pretended to quiver in fear.

Once the table was set, they all sat down and began to catch up. Stacey couldn't shake the feeling that something was missing, but it took her several minutes to figure out what that something was. 'Did you guys stop drinking wine?"

Angie smiled with a flush in her cheeks. "Well, this stays between us for now, but I'm pregnant."

"Oh my God," Stacey squealed and embraced her sister-in-law before leaning over to punch Gavin in the shoulder harder than she normally would. "You shit! You never told me you were trying."

"We weren't," he said pointedly and rubbed his shoulder.

"It was a surprise." Angie winked at her.

"How far along are you?"

"Well, I haven't had a sonogram, but I'm thinking about six weeks."

"That's incredible. I'm so happy for you guys."

There was a moment of silence while they ate, and Stacey tried to find a way to lead into her mission.

"What do you want?" Gavin asked.

"Hmm?"

"You've got that shit-eating, no nonsense look you get when you want someone to do something for you. It's like instead of being caught with your hand in the cookie jar, you're trying to talk someone into the opening the jar for you."

"So, I need a favor," she gently began. "I have to go to Boston to follow up on a lead for my story."

"Did you get moved to the case for those missing girls?" Angie asked.

Stacey shook her head. "Mike says we don't have reason to cover it. It's outside our range. I'm still pissed about that one."

"So, it's the car then?" Gavin asked as he swirled pasta onto his fork. "Everyone's been talking about it."

She nodded. "Yeah. It hasn't been announced publicly yet, but it's tied to a missing person's case from the '90s. The woman is from Boston."

"How do you know that?"

"Easton Gates told me," She said without thinking before her eyes went wide. "And don't you dare tell anyone I told you that. He could get in trouble."

"Like I care," he snorted. "So, what does this have to do with me?"

"I'll need you to check on Mom and Dad while I'm gone."

"Oh, for the love of—" Gavin slammed down his fork.

"It's only for a couple of days."

"Isn't Mom back on her feet?"

"She's doing a lot better, but she's still on the weak side and Dad can't handle everything on his own."

"They've been playing you, Stacey."

"I can't deal with the drama right now. It's only for a couple of days. Besides, you owe me."

"How the hell do I owe you?"

"Umm, what about you coming to the house the morning after I broke down and telling them I was seeing things?"

"You were."

"So, it was late and dark, and I saw wrong. Was there really a need to tell them I hallucinated and have them start hounding me about my job? Again?"

Gavin sighed. "Okay. Maybe it was an asshole move. I'm sorry. I was scared for you. I wanted to check on you. But then they got pushy about what happened to make me need to check

Disappearance on Route 6

on you. It slipped out. I wasn't thinking. You know how they can get."

"I understand that. But at least do me a solid on this to make up for it."

"How long are you going to be gone?"

"Hopefully a day. Two at the most. Just check in on them in the morning and around seven at night to make sure Mom takes her pills and help her to bed."

Gavin sighed and ran his fingers through his hair.

Angie glanced between them. "I could look in on them for you."

"Thanks, but you know how they are. You're a sore spot with them. With Mom's health the way it is, it should be Gavin."

Angie responded by studying her plate quietly.

"Damn it, Stacey. You know I can't deal with them."

"Yet you're okay sending your wife into the lion's den?"

"Fine. Fine."

"Love you, bro."

"So, why exactly are you going to Boston if this woman's missing?"

"The husband is still there. I'm hoping to get the inside scoop before someone else. This could be the big break I need."

"Your boss is okay with this?" Angie asked.

"As long as I get him something to print."

The next morning, Stacey pulled up in front of a beautiful brick colonial style home. The front porch was large and inviting and the wide windows were the perfect frame.

She approached the door confidently and rang the bell. She immediately felt sympathy for the man who opened the door.

His hair was thinning and gray, and his blue eyes, swimming with sadness, hid behind dark circles.

"Mr. Patterson?"

"Yes."

"Hi, my name is Stacey Branch." She extended her hand for him to shake. "I'm sorry to show up on your doorstep like this, but I have some news that seemed inappropriate to share over the phone."

"What's that?"

"It's regarding your wife Susanna and your children."

He closed his eyes tightly and took a deep breath. "They're dead, aren't they?"

"What? No. I mean, I don't know. I'm here to tell you Susanna's car was found."

He gave her a long stare and then stood back to allow her to come inside. She followed him into a living space with marble floors and mahogany furniture. He sank down into a plush chair, and she sat opposite him.

"Are you with the police?" He asked her.

"No. I'm a newspaper reporter. I'm honestly surprised the police haven't contacted you about this already."

He scoffed. "They barely investigated. They were quick to rule it as a voluntary disappearance but that never made any sense. Susanna was not the kind to worry her family. There's no way in hell she dropped off the face of the planet by choice. Where was the car found?"

"In DeSoto, Virginia. It was discovered submerged in the lake by a couple of fishermen."

"But they weren't—"

"There were no bodies inside," she said gently.

He nodded and then blew out his breath.

"I was able to trace the car to your wife's case, but I don't have a lot of the information."

"That doesn't surprise me. She was traced to DeSoto but then everything went cold."

"Why was she there?"

"Oh god," David rubbed his eyes before continuing. "I'm not proud of this, but I had an affair right before she left. She walked in on us. She took the kids and headed out to see her sister. They disappeared on the way."

"Where does her sister live?"

"Georgia. I waited several days to call. I wanted to give her space, and Mallory never liked me, but when I called, I was told they never showed up. Mallory wasn't even expecting her. She was as floored as me."

Stacey pulled out a notebook to write all this down. "They traced her to DeSoto through credit card receipts?"

"They started the process for that, but I actually got a phone call from her that pushed things forward."

This surprised Stacey. She hadn't seen anything like this through everything she'd read and watched. "A phone call?"

He nodded. "She called me the morning after I reported her missing. She was hysterical and not making a lot of sense. She told me she was at the Seaside Motel, and someone tried to kill her and had taken the kids. While I was trying to get more info out of her, she told me she could hear the person outside. I instructed her to hide and immediately called the detective in charge of her case."

"Was this detective with the FBI?"

David shook his head. "No. At least I don't think so. He didn't say he was, and he wasn't wearing an FBI vest like you see on TV. He showed up like an hour after I made the call."

Stacey made a note about the detective and decided to go back to the conversation, as the image of the blood-like substance in the closet was clear in her mind. "Okay. Back to Susanna's phone call. Did she give a name or description of the person she said took her?"

"No," he shook his head, "but she did say it was the same guy who helped her when she broke down on the road. He apparently followed her to the hotel. Anyway, the detective called the police there to send a cruiser out, and he immediately flew out to investigate himself. They found nothing. A couple of weeks later, I was told Susanna was clearly angry about the affair and took off with the kids. They believed the phone call was made up to scare me as revenge."

"So, they had no evidence she was there?"

"No, she was there," he answered. "Her last credit card charge was to the motel, but the charge was made a week before her phone call to me, and she didn't stay there long. They traced the phone records, and she did call me from the motel. But she wasn't there when the police arrived and there was no sign of a struggle or that they'd been there at all."

Stacey let out a snort of derision, prompting David's confusion.

"What?" he asked. "Is that wrong?"

"I shouldn't say."

"Please," his voice was pained.

"A lot of people could get in trouble if I tell you. I'm not even supposed to know the things I do."

"I would never tell anyone your name," he pleaded. "I need closure. Please. This is my family."

She nodded. "My methods of investigating are a bit unorthodox. I broke into the motel and found plenty to suggest your family was there. There was a stain in a closet in the office that looked like blood. It hasn't been confirmed yet. It's with the lab now. I also found a blanket in the lost and found that was dated the day after they were checked in. And—"

Stacey paused before reaching into her bag and pulling out the stuffed dog, still in its evidence baggie. She handed it to David and his eyes immediately welled up.

"It's Sparky," he whispered.

"Pardon?"

"Sparky. This was Bethany's favorite toy. She never went anywhere without him. If it's not with her—" he choked up and grabbed a tissue off the coffee table. "Where was he?"

"Under the bed in the room they stayed in," she said quietly.

"Honey, I'm going to the store to get Jake some jeans for school!"

There was a click clack of heels on the floor seconds before a woman walked into the room. She was blonde and wore a red dress, and heels. "Oh! David, are you okay?"

"Yeah," he said, wiping his eyes. "This is Stacey Branch. Miss Branch, this is my wife, Tia. Miss Branch is an investigative reporter. She came to tell me Susanna's car was found."

"Oh!" Tia exclaimed and put a hand to her chest. "Wow, after all this time. Are they okay?"

"Susanna and the children haven't been located yet, I'm afraid," Stacey told her.

"Oh, what a shame," she said before turning back to David. "I have to go get Jake new jeans. Are you going to be okay?"

"Yeah, I'm okay," he smiled at her.

"Okay, I'll be back soon," she squeezed his hand before heading for the front door.

Stacey waited until she heard the front door close before continuing to speak. "I realize this is probably a lot to take in after all this time."

"You've done more than anyone else has," he told her. "I can't believe the police haven't even told me they found the car."

"So, I have a question that may help the investigation. It's going to sound somewhat insensitive though."

"Anything you need. I want my children back. Susanna too. I mean, we had our problems, and our marriage was in trouble, but I never wanted anything bad to happen to her."

"Well, that stain in the closet—" she said gently. "My contact at the lab said he'll be able to tell if it's blood but not if it's one of theirs unless he has DNA to compare it to."

"DNA? After twenty-six years? Is that possible?"

"I think it depends on what it is. Do you still have their things?"

He hesitated for a moment and then rose to his feet, gesturing for her to follow him down a long hallway.

"Tia and I compromised. When we got married, she wanted me to get rid of everything, but I couldn't bring myself to do it.

So, we put everything in one room so she wouldn't have to see it."

He opened a door on the left and allowed Stacey to step into the room. "I can't come in here anymore. Whenever I try, it awakens too many emotions. I'll let you look around."

He immediately stepped out of the room and shut the door behind him, leaving Stacey alone.

She glanced around the room and couldn't help but feel emotion as she glanced over the items. Toddler mattresses leaned against the wall. Toys were everywhere.

Stacey made her way to a dresser in the corner and slowly rifled through the drawers. She was hesitant to grab clothes, but there was no telling what else may be there.

In the bottom drawer she found two scrapbooks and flipped through the pages. She quickly discovered they were the baby books documenting the first year of each of the kids' lives. Her heart skipped a beat to see a lock of hair in Mason's book with the caption, *Baby's first haircut!* Then she flipped through Bethany's book and was ecstatic to see a lock of her hair as well. What luck!

She checked a few more areas before finding a hairbrush with strands of hair still in it in a drawer in a bedside table.

Stacey made her way back down the hall and found David sitting in the living room with his head in his hands. "Mr. Patterson?"

He turned to her.

She held up the items she found. "I found the kids' baby books. There's hair in them. That may work. There was also a brush with Susanna's hair in it."

"The baby books?"

There was so much pain in his voice that she was overcome with the urge to rush forward and embrace him, but she choked it down, not wanting to be weird.

"I'll be careful with them and return them to you when I'm done. I promise."

He nodded as the tears flowed freely down his face.

"Do you still have contact information for Susanna's sister?"

"I haven't talked to her in years," he answered. "I don't know if anything's changed, but I'll get your what I have."

He rose from his chair and walked through a door on the opposite side of the room.

CHAPTER SEVEN

Stacey's flight for Georgia didn't leave until eleven twenty in the evening. She spent the rest of her time in the airport sending off emails and writing an early article to send to her boss.

Once she'd done all that, she looked up hotels near the airport in Georgia. She knew the time she arrived would not be appropriate to show up at Mallory's home. Plus, she was extremely tired and needed a few hours' sleep at least.

She scrolled through a list of hotels in the nearby area and was discouraged to see they were all either closed or full. Finally, she came across the listing for a bed-and-breakfast that was slightly out of the way, but it wasn't too horrible of a drive. She couldn't find a button to book online so she called the number listed.

"Hello. Blackwood Manor Bed & Breakfast."

"Hi. I tried to book online but couldn't find a link."

"I'm so sorry about that. The links tend to break. We're working on it. When were you wanting to book for?"

"Well, my flight will be leaving any minute from Boston, and I plan on coming straight there from the airport. Probably sometime around three a.m. Do you have any openings? The website says you do."

"We have one room empty right now. Chances are no one will come in before you get here but we can't hold it without a credit card. We can either do it now to hold the room or you can wait until you come in. It's your choice."

"Let's go ahead and handle it now." She gave the person her credit card information and hung up as her flight was being called to board.

"They drove me nuts!" Gavin complained through the Bluetooth connection in the rental car.

"Uh huh," Stacey said as she scrutinized the GPS screen. Blackwood Manor would be coming up on her right in about five minutes, and she wanted to make sure she didn't miss the drive.

"Are you listening to me?"

"Gavin, look," she snapped, exasperated. "It's three o'clock in the morning. I've barely slept. I had to drive out of my way by about twenty minutes to find a place to sleep. I have an important story to cover that could make or break my career, and I regularly take care of Mom and Dad. Forgive me if I don't give a shit about your complaints from a single day."

"That's different. You're the golden child. They hate me."

"They do not hate you."

"Dad does. Did you forget he stuck me in juvie?"

"Did you forget you stole his truck?"

"I went for a joy ride! Like every other normal teenager out there. It did not call for that."

"So, what the hell did they do to warrant you calling me six times while I was getting a rental car?"

"Mom knocked my beer out of my hand during dinner."

"Oh, the horror."

"AND she insisted on checking my teeth after I brushed them to make sure I got them good enough. I'm thirty years old, and my mommy is checking my teeth."

"Okay, that's pretty bad."

"Oh, that's not the worst of it. Dad told me I still had time to be reinstated in the will. All I have to do is divorce Angie before children come into the equation."

"Good God."

"I can't do this much longer, Stace. It's only a matter of time before they figure out she's pregnant, and I'm not looking forward to the war. I don't have your patience. When are you coming home?"

She sighed. "I have to get a shower and a few hours' sleep. I'm going to talk to my source as early as I possibly can. Depending on how that goes, probably late tonight. But it will be after dinner."

"Damn it, Stacey."

"These things can't be helped, bro. Oh, hold up. I think I see the place I'm gonna be staying."

She came to a stop and stared at a large, white plantation home in the distance. There were lights dancing in the windows emitting a somewhat eerie glow over the land.

"Weird. It's creepy and beautiful at the same time."

"Like Mom and Dad."

"Shut up. I have to go."

She hung up the phone and pulled into the drive, which was lined with gorgeous trees until she reached a small parking area. She grabbed her suitcase and made her way up to the front door.

She opened the door a crack and stuck her head inside. There was a podium set up next to a grand staircase. A man smiled at her and set down his magazine.

"I've never stayed in a bed-and-breakfast before," she said nervously. "Do I come in?"

"Yes, yes. Please, come in."

She stepped into the entryway and closed the door behind her. The place was grand and beautiful, but her stomach did somersaults, and she instantly felt sorrow.

"Miss Branch?"

"Yes, that's me."

"Okay, I'll need you to sign here," he said placing a piece of paper in front of her. "We serve breakfast at seven, but I'm assuming you won't be up that early. If you want, we can have something sent to your room a little later."

"That would be great. Maybe around nine?"

"Can do." He handed her a pamphlet. "I'll show you upstairs," he said as he rounded the podium.

"That's okay. You can give me the key. I'll find it."

"Oh, we don't have keys. I'll need to show you where the bathroom is anyway."

"You don't have keys? That seems a little weird."

"You can lock your room from the inside."

"Yeah, but like what if there's an emergency? You know, like a fire, or someone is hurt or sick?"

"The owner has a master key that has access to all the rooms in the event of an emergency, but we don't have traditional room keys."

"What did you mean you have to show me the bathroom? There's no bathroom in the room?"

"This used to be a plantation home. There are not bathrooms attached to each bedroom. Everyone on the floor shares one."

Stacey was filled with anxiety. Something here didn't seem right. She didn't know what normal bed-and-breakfast etiquette was, but this magnificent building felt like a vessel for doom.

The man seemed to sense her distress and said, "If you want to cancel, I'd be happy to refund your card in full."

"No, everywhere close is booked, and I desperately need sleep. I'll do it. It's one night."

"Alright." He led her up the stairs and to the right. "This here is the bathroom. Your bedroom is on the opposite side of the hall, last door on the right. You'll find fresh towels inside."

"Thank you. What about Wi-Fi? I completely forgot to ask on the phone."

"Password is on that pamphlet I gave you."

"Awesome. Thank you."

"No problem," he told her before descending the stairs.

Stacey walked down the hall and peeked inside the door on the right. She found an ordinary bedroom. There was a queen-sized bed, two bedside tables, and a dresser along one wall with white, fluffy towels sitting atop it. There was a small desk opposite the bed with a TV mounted above it.

It would do.

Stacey wheeled her suitcase inside it, grabbed a couple of towels and headed back down to the bathroom.

The bathroom was a small room with a claw-foot bathtub, which she found particularly intriguing. The water pressure wasn't the best, but she couldn't deny how good it felt loosening up the tension-filled knots of travel.

A giggle tore across the room that made her blood run cold despite the hot water. "Hello?"

She held her breath and carefully watched the curtain where a shadow quickly darted from one side to the other. Stacey shut off the water and tore open the curtain. There was no one in the room and the door was tightly closed.

Her heart pounded dangerously in her chest. Her anxiety had been building from the moment she'd landed, though she couldn't explain why. There was an uneasiness in this house. No. She was tired. She grabbed her towel to dry off before quickly dressing and heading back to her room. She fell asleep before her head hit the pillow.

"Well, well, aren't you pretty?" Stacey woke up to a small voice a few feet away and felt pressure near her feet in the bed.

She opened her eyes and was startled to see a young child sitting cross-legged at the foot of the bed. Her immediate reaction was anger at another guest's child sneaking into her room. This is why there should be room keys! Then she noticed the girl's appearance. She wore a white gown with an obvious blood stain across the front, slightly blue and scaly skin, and nubs on her forehead.

Stacey's breath caught for a moment, and she nearly screamed, but the child's demeanor stopped her. She wasn't being menacing at all. She didn't smile. Her eyes were filled with sadness, and Stacey wanted to reach out and embrace her.

"Who are you?"

"Lucy," the girl said simply, as though no further explanation was needed.

"What do you want?"

Lucy sighed before staring deeply into her eyes. "Do you know what I don't understand? The mentality that so many have that dying will end pain. That's so wrong. I've never hurt more."

Stacey was captivated by this child. She was small in stature—no older than eight at the most, but she spoke so eloquently. It was as though her body stopped growing at the time of her death, but her mind continued to blossom over the years.

"You're the first person I've been able to talk to in so long. Well, other than Emily."

"Emily."

"The owner's daughter. It won't last though. Children outgrow their openness." She sighed. "You though? I sensed something special in you the minute you walked through the door. I thought I'd talk and see if you acknowledged me."

"Why can I see you?"

"This house pulls in those with special gifts. Do you have one?"

Stacey shook her head.

"Are you sure about that?"

Stacey looked back over her life. She tended to know things she shouldn't—something that drove her father up a wall. She'd seen Susanna Patterson down Route 6 twice when she hadn't been there. Maybe she did have a gift.

Lucy nodded knowingly. "I'm something like you, I think. If I'd grown up, we could have been mirror sisters."

"You don't even know me."

"I know more than you think. I know your soul. Those you seek are still alive, you know."

Stacey's pulse quickened. "How can you possibly know that?"

"Energy. You are a perceptive person. Your gift is proof of it. Don't shut it out. You can only succeed if you let it in. Don't let others squander your shine. If you do, you'll end up alone."

"You seem sure of that."

She snorted. "Mommy issues recognize mommy issues."

CHAPTER EIGHT

Stacey woke up to knocking on her door. "Miss Branch," a voice called out. "You requested a meal at 9 a.m.?"

She rose from the bed and took a breakfast tray from a smiling woman. As she dug into her meal, she logged onto her laptop. There was a response from her email to Marjorie Swanson agreeing to talk on the phone later. She was surprised, however, to see the email from her father.

Stacey,

What do you mean by taking off to Boston like that without telling us? Your brother is upsetting your mother. A little notice would have been nice. Also, travelling to a place like that alone is not smart. Do you know how much crime they have? You should have gone with a coworker or even your brother's wife.

Now that your article is out, you have a target on your back. You need to come home so you can be protected. I implore you.

Your father.

Whoa, whoa, whoa. Pump the brakes. Her father emailed her? Her father? The man knew nothing about technology. He would have somehow had to get her email address, go into the library, and create an account. Someone would have to show him how. He must really be worried about her. If they had a phone, she'd call to reassure him she was okay, but she couldn't get them to agree to one.

She closed the laptop and downed the last of the steaming coffee in her mug. It was time to get going.

An hour later she pulled up to a trailer home. It was one of the best kept in the little community. The lawn was green and freshly grown, and there was a new deck leading up to the door.

She knocked on the door and was blown away when it was opened. The woman on the other side appeared older than her, but the family resemblance was remarkable.

"Mallory?

The woman nodded. "Are you Stacey?"

Stacey's mouth dropped open in shock. She hadn't called ahead. Was this woman a mind reader?

The shock must have been evident on her face because Mallory gave her a small smile. "David called me."

Stacey relaxed. "Oh. Yes. Yes, I am."

Mallory stepped to the side so she could come inside. She offered a beverage, and Stacey took a seat on the couch and observed her surroundings while she waited for Mallory to come back.

"I'm surprised you're here already. I wasn't expecting you so soon. David said you were there yesterday morning."

"I went straight to the airport from his house," Stacey agreed as she took a can of soda.

"You must have got in late. Where did you stay?"

"Bed and breakfast outside of town. Blackwood something."

Mallory's jaw dropped. "And you made it through the night? You must be special."

"What do you mean?"

"It's notoriously haunted. It was vacant for years because no one would go near it. The new owners turned it into a bed-and-breakfast. Most people around here still won't go near it. I definitely won't. I mean, it's gorgeous, but I don't need that bad juju."

Oh wow, Stacey thought to herself. *If I lived here this place would make a great story.*

"Well, I was so tired I wouldn't have noticed a ghost if it smacked me in the face," Stacey joked.

Mallory laughed. "So, David said you found Susanna's car." Her expression turned sad as she said the words.

"We did," Stacey said gently. "There was no sign of them though."

Mallory nodded in understanding. "Still, it's more than we've ever gotten before. It doesn't look good." She sighed. "I'm not sure what I can do to help you, but I'll do anything I can."

"I'm surprised you talked to David. He mentioned you hadn't spoken in years."

"We hadn't. We worked together in the beginning. I flew out there a few times, and he came here. We went anywhere we could think of she might be. Her favorite places, things that lined up with her interests. We banded together when the police said she ran off. We both knew better. But it was dead end after dead end, and we gave up and stopped talking. We never got along before, so it didn't make sense to keep in contact."

"Why didn't you get along?"

"I always thought he was too slick. This picture of perfect, and let's face it, no one's perfect. I felt like there was some hidden person under the surface, and I didn't want that for Susanna. I knew he'd end up hurting her."

"When she went missing, did you think he did something to her?"

"No, no," Mallory shook her head. "Nothing like that. He never laid a hand on her, and she would have told me if he did. Plus, the kids were gone too. David was a good father. He worshipped those kids. It's the one thing I did like about him."

"So, he was never a suspect?" She hadn't seen anything during her research to indicate he had been, which surprised her. Typically, in a missing person's case, the spouse was the number one suspect.

"He was. Briefly. The detective told me they were investigating him because he was having an affair, and Susanna found out. But they were able to verify through phone records that she called him after she was reported missing from another state. That basically cleared his name."

"Did you talk to her beforehand?"

"Yes and no. I knew they were having problems. I talked to her a couple of weeks before that. She cried and told me she was thinking about leaving him. I told her not to do anything rash and maybe she needed time away to cool down. She did mention coming to see me soon with the kids, but we didn't actively plan anything, and I had no idea she was on her way. David called one night demanding to talk to her and I was so confused. When it finally clicked that neither of us knew where she was, the bottom dropped out of my stomach."

"Why did she drive?"

"She had a fear of flying," Mallory chuckled half-heartedly. "It's ironic, isn't it? She was so scared of flying. She drove everywhere. But it was a drive where something awful happened."

"Did she ever make that drive before?"

"Yes. About twice a year. When I went to visit her, I'd fly, but she could probably do the drive in her sleep."

"Did she always stop in the same places?"

"Usually. The police said the hotel she normally stayed at was closed that night due to a water main break."

"That's really interesting." She meant it. Susanna deviating from her routine could be the key to finding out how everything unraveled. "What do you believe her next move would be?"

"Knowing Susanna, she would likely try to push through until her next scheduled stop, a 24-hour pancake house. There was also a hotel across the street from it. She would have tried to kill two birds with one stone."

"Okay, so where was this?"

"Abington, Virginia."

"Abington?" A lightbulb went off in Stacey's mind.

"Yeah. Why?" Mallory narrowed her eyes in frustration.

"I'm not sure yet," Stacey answered honestly. "That's roughly three hours from DeSoto. She was close to her destination. I'm wondering what veered her off track. I'll investigate it."

"Well, her car wasn't in the best shape. She'd been trying to talk David into getting a new one for a while, but he wanted to wait."

"He did tell me she mentioned breaking down when she called him on the phone."

Mallory nodded. "He told me the same thing. Could she have been trying to find a mechanic?"

Stacey shook her head. "I doubt it. DeSoto is in the middle of nowhere. There is a used car shop there, but the chances she'd go there instead of to one of the bigger cities—"

Mallory's gaze fell to the floor.

"Don't worry," Stacey said sweetly and reached over to squeeze the woman's hand. "This is a good detail. She went off course. There was a reason why, and I will be investigating that. Remember, I live right outside DeSoto. I plan on travelling all the different routes to see if I can find something that makes sense."

"Thank you." Mallory smiled gratefully.

Stacey smiled back before returning to her notes.

"Did anyone ever talk to David's mistress? Did that ever come out publicly?"

"I'm pretty sure that information was never released since it was determined that Susanna left of her own accord, but he ended up marrying her."

Stacey dropped her notebook. "What?"

"He married her. After he was granted a divorce from Susanna. I found it grimy personally. This woman was the reason Susanna was on the road that night and he marries her. He told me during the investigation he felt guilty about the whole thing, but he couldn't have felt too guilty."

Stacey wrote Tia's name in big, bold letters on her notepad and circled it. She would need to explore that angle more.

"Did you ever meet her?"

Mallory snorted. "Yeah. The last time I saw David. It turned out Susanna had a storage unit, and she'd paid up for a while, but they eventually called for payment. He didn't want to keep it, so he signed it over to me. I went out there to clear it out and that bitch hovered the whole time we were doing paperwork. I asked her if she had a problem, and she said she wanted to make sure I wasn't going to cheat David out of anything. I told her she killed my sister, niece, and nephew and she had no business accusing anyone else of cheating anything. She got huffy, and the guy who ran the place said we couldn't both stay. David was originally going to help me, but he left with her."

"Was there anything unusual about the storage unit?"

"There wasn't a lot in it. It was a big unit like maybe she anticipated filling it up with more, but there were only a few boxes of mementos from our childhood and a couple of pieces of furniture."

"Does the unit still exist?"

Mallory shook her head. "No. I cleaned it out that day. Arranged for a thrift store to pick up the furniture and shipped the boxes back home. It only took a couple of hours."

"Alright, Mallory," Stacey slipped her notepad into her bag. "That's all the questions I have for now. I appreciate you taking the time to talk to me. If I have any more questions through the course of my investigation, can I call you?"

"Please," Mallory smiled. "And—" Her smile faltered as she paused.

"What is it?" Stacey asked genuinely.

"Well, would you mind keeping me in the loop on everything? Not only if you have questions but about the things you find? Maybe even call to—" She closed her eyes and blushed. "I'm not explaining this well. My children are grown now, and they rarely call. I don't have Susanna anymore. You're easy to talk to. I know you're a reporter, and I should be cautious about what I tell you but, I don't know, I feel like I've known you all my life."

Stacey nodded. She'd been told this before. She didn't know what it was about her, but people tended to rip their hearts open and pour their souls onto her shoes without even knowing her. She didn't mind though. Helping people was something she thoroughly enjoyed.

"Of course I will."

The two women exchanged their goodbyes and as she walked back out to her rental car her cell phone rang.

"Hello," Stacey said as she slipped behind the wheel.

"Stacey!" Elinor's panicked voice exclaimed. "Do you know when you're coming back?"

"I just got done talking to Susanna's sister. I'm about to find somewhere to ship some stuff back and then head to the airport. Not sure when the next flight is though. Why? What's up?"

"Something's happened," Elinor exhaled, and Stacey could hear her trying to control her breathing. "Another woman's gone missing."

"Mike won't let us touch that."

"It's closer to home."

"In Logan's Ridge?"

"Yes."

"Okay. Well, let Mike know I'm on my way. I'll be there as soon as I can."

"He already put Marcy on it."

Stacey was a little shocked to hear this. "Marcy's the gossip columnist. It's not going to take me long."

"Well, he can't put you on this. We think it might be related to the story you're working on."

"Ellie, those girls started getting snatched a year before Susanna's car was found."

"I can't say over the phone, Stace. But it is related to your case. Get home."

"All the more reason for me to start as soon as possible."

Elinor cleared her throat but then there was a moment of silence and Stacey knew she was trying to choose her next words carefully.

"Ellie, what the hell is going on?"

"Stacey, it's your sister-in-law."

CHAPTER NINE

Stacey raced to Gavin's apartment as soon as she landed. When he opened the door, his eyes were bloodshot and there were dried tears all down his face. He immediately pulled her into his arms and sobbed.

She stepped inside the apartment and shut the door behind her. "What happened?" she asked him.

He stepped back and moved to sit on the sofa. It was then Stacey noticed how messy the apartment was. There was dirty laundry everywhere, and the coffee table was littered with cans. Angie normally kept the place impeccably clean. When she'd been here a couple of nights before, the apartment was like something out of a magazine.

"Well, I was at Mom and Dad's last night and Angie called me. They were pissed I took a call, but I knew if she was calling me while I was there, it was important. So, I'm trying to talk with her and them at the same time, and it ends up being a shouting match. Angie told me not to come home, so I stayed over there in my old room. I was on my way to work this morning when I got a call. It sounded like Angie was fighting with someone. She never actually spoke to me. I don't know if it was a butt dial or what. But she was clearly struggling. I came straight here, and she was gone. The bedroom has blood all over the floor."

His voice and shoulders shook, and Stacey eyed the destroyed living room. "Was the place like this before?"

He nodded. "Yeah. It's been getting out of control."

Stacey was a little shocked to hear him say that. How had it gotten so out of control in a couple of days?

"What were you guys fighting about?"

"Something about the pregnancy. I was having a hard time understanding her with Mom and Dad sniping away in my other ear. They heard the word 'baby', and everything blew up like I knew it would. Dad was talking about how irresponsible I am, and how she wouldn't be a fit mother. Out loud, I said everyone needed to shut up and let me think. She ended up snapping at me that I clearly sided with my father and if I can't stand up for her to stay there. But I *did* stand up for her. I did."

"Gavin," Stacey said gently. "Are you happy about this baby?"

She wasn't an idiot. It hadn't escaped her attention that he didn't smile or have much to say when Angie told her the other night.

"It's hard, Stace," he admitted. "We weren't trying, so it was a shock. We never talked about having kids. Then I can't help but wonder if I'd pass the toxicity down."

"What do you mean?"

Gavin sneered. "Look who raised us. We were suffocated as hell. I don't want to put my kid through that. I never want to make anyone feel the way that I—"

He cried harder, and Stacey sat down next to him and put her arm around his shoulders.

It was a lot to take in. Their parents were never fans of Angie. She grew up on the wild side, and they considered her to be a heathen.

Gavin and Angie met in juvie when he did his short stint for stealing their father's truck. Angie was in for a little longer. Her mother died when she was young, and her father basically ignored her. She acted out a lot trying to get his attention, and he put her in saying she was out of control. He never came back for her.

She'd had to stay until a foster placement was found for her, where she remained until she aged out of the system. Most people were sympathetic to Angie's circumstances and didn't judge her but Paul and Alice, especially Paul, believed she was a bad seed. They hadn't wanted them to move in together, and they sure as hell hadn't wanted them to get married. Stacey could imagine they would lose their minds at Angie being pregnant.

"Could you make out any part of the conversation on the phone? Or recognize any voices?"

He shook his head. "It was muffled like the phone was in her pocket. Her voice was strained like she was upset, and it sounded like she screamed a couple of times."

"Did the neighbors hear anything?"

"If they did, they're not talking. The police went door to door, and everyone claims they weren't home at the time of the phone call."

Gavin opened his mouth to say something else but was cut off by an authoritative knock on the door.

Stacey went to answer it and stepped aside to let Easton Gates and another police officer inside.

Easton nodded but didn't speak to her. Instead, he strode across the room to stand in front of Gavin. "Mr. Branch, we need you to come down to the station with us for questioning."

Gavin's eyebrows wrinkled. "What? Why?"

"We tracked your wife's cell phone."

"Did you find her?"

"No, but we found her phone where we traced it to. The auto shop where you work."

Stacey stared at Gavin. Angie was at his job? Why? Why did he say she was at home?

"No." Gavin shook his head. "You have it wrong. Angie had no reason to be there. I was on my way to work when I got the call, and I turned around. There's blood in the bedroom."

"That's why you need to come in for questioning."

"But—"

"Mr. Branch, if you do not come willingly, we will be forced to get an arrest warrant to compel you."

Gavin's jaw hung open and he whipped around to her. "Stacey?"

She shook her head. "Get up, Gavin. You have to go with them. The faster you do, the faster we can get this whole thing cleared up."

He rose to his feet and walked past Easton toward his partner and the door. Easton came to a stop next to Stacey. "Miss Branch, maybe you ought to come too."

Stacey was getting restless two hours later as she sat in the hot interrogation room of the police station. When the door opened, she sat up quickly and narrowed her eyes at Easton as he entered the room.

"I'm sorry for the wait," he told her as he slipped a can of soda her direction.

"What are we doing here?" she asked him simply. "Are we in trouble for something?"

"Well, as I said back at your brother's apartment, we traced his wife's cell phone to his place of employment. It was found on his work bench, which shows he may have seen her. We're trying to get to the bottom of everything."

"Well, I've been out of town for a couple of days. I don't know how to help you."

"Oh, I know you've been out of town," he told her as he leaned back in his chair. His expression was much more serious than the last time she'd seen him. There was no hint of a smirk on his lips, and his eyes were cloudy. "I asked you here to talk about something else."

"Okay?" she said as she narrowed her eyebrows in confusion.

"Your article made for interesting reading material," he told her.

Her stomach clenched, and she fought the urge to look away from that icy stare of his. She'd been dreading this moment.

"You told me you weren't going to put anything I told you in print."

Her gaze flickered to the two-way mirror, but he snapped his fingers in front of her face, jerking her attention back to him. "There's no one listening. It's you and me. For now. So, look at me."

"I didn't put what you told me in print."

"The hell you didn't."

"Technically, I didn't," she pressed on. "You refused to tell names. I figured it out on my own. Technically, I printed what I found out."

His stare could have burned a vampire. "Seriously?"

"It is public information."

"It is. But did you stop to think for even one minute they'd wonder how you knew to look in that direction? We were seen together that same day, Stacey. My ass is in the hot seat."

She hadn't thought of that. But at the end of the day, she didn't feel she was wrong. "I didn't. I'm sorry about that, but I'm not sorry I wrote the article."

He tapped his fingertips on the table, and his lips tightened even more.

"Look at it from my perspective," she told him. "Susanna's case didn't get enough attention at the time. It was barely investigated and wasn't even in any local papers. Hell, it doesn't even seem like the FBI ever got involved. Sure, Boston ran the story for a few months, but not here. That family deserves to know what happened."

"We don't know what happened," he told her.

"And we never will if no one takes the time to investigate."

"There are things about this case you don't know."

"I think I know more than you on the subject."

He glared at her. "That's a big statement to make. Police are investigating what happened to her. Just because we aren't sharing every little detail with the press doesn't mean nothing is being done."

"Nothing was done back then. How am I supposed to believe something will be done this time?"

"There was no evidence of foul play at the time," he said through gritted teeth. "The car being found obviously changes that. The case has been reopened, and we are working with Boston P.D. That does not go to print. Do you understand me?"

"Well, it is nice to know someone is finally taking this thing seriously."

"You are infuriating, woman," he growled.

She shrugged her shoulders and gave him a sweet smile.

"Where were you? When we reached out to the newspaper, we were told you were out of town on assignment."

"I went to speak to the victim's family."

He stared at her incredulously. "You went to Boston?"

She nodded. "And to Georgia."

"They didn't think it was strange a reporter showed up asking questions?"

"Please. They practically treated me as a therapist. I guess letting them know the car was found gave me their trust."

"Why did you tell them that?"

"Because it *was*."

"For your information, we were waiting until we had more evidence to go on before telling the family. We didn't want them getting their hopes up."

"Well, they were relieved to get the information, so I'd say I made the right call."

"And if we never find anything else? How's it going to feel knowing you reopened an old wound and now they're waiting for the phone to ring?"

She shook her head at him. "You dumb son of a bitch."

"Excuse me?"

"You can't reopen a wound that never closed to begin with."

He chose to ignore her statement and leaned in toward her. "I'm telling you. Let this go. It's dangerous. You revealed your cards too early. You should have waited for the police to make a statement. Now whoever has done this knows you know too much. I guarantee that's why Angie was snatched."

"Hmm. And what about the six girls last year? Were they snatched because I was getting too close to something?"

"We don't have reason to believe she was taken by the same person. The evidence points to it being personal to *you*. You need to sit back, keep your mouth shut, and stop printing shit that has not been released."

She leaned in toward him, a clear sign she was not being intimidated. "Freedom of the press, Easton. I will do whatever it takes to find out what happened to these people and get that family closure."

"Even if it puts a target on your back?"

"Even if. Am I under arrest?"

He gave her one last pointed stare. "No."

"Then we're done here." She rose to her feet and stormed out the door behind him.

CHAPTER TEN

"Can you believe him?" Stacey thundered as she slammed the coffeepot back into place. When she'd left the police station, she'd gone straight to the newspaper office where she'd researched and written for a couple of hours. Now she was on break with Elinor and gave her the run-down of everything that happened in the past few days.

"Well, yeah," Elinor said sympathetically.

"What?" Stacey glared at her.

"He could lose his job."

"But all he told me was it belonged to a missing person. He didn't give me a name."

"No, but he told you it was a woman with children from Boston. That narrows the field considerably."

"El, come on," Stacey rolled her eyes.

"I'm not saying you shouldn't investigate. But maybe you should've waited until the police announced it to put it in print."

"I had to print something," Stacey protested as she took a sip of her coffee. "My article was due."

"It could have been the basics of the car being found. You know. Like the other papers did."

"The other papers?" Stacey's eyes flashed with fury. "You're the one that told me how this is my big story."

"It is! But there are ways to do things. I don't think he was trying to intimidate you. He could be right. You printed something that, by all intents and purposes, you shouldn't know. That's going to freak out the person responsible. We think that's why your sister-in-law was taken. In fact, Mike talked about taking you off the story altogether."

"What?" Stacey exclaimed and slammed her coffee mug down on the table. "He can't do that!"

"Oh, relax. You've been back at work for a couple of hours. I'm sure he decided against it. But you have to admit, you wrote this article, and Angie immediately goes missing. Plus, we got some disturbing phone calls while you were gone."

"Disturbing how?"

"Well, the phone on your desk was relentlessly ringing, so I picked it up and there was a man on the line asking to speak to you. I told him you were away on assignment, and he asked where. I told him I couldn't divulge that information, and he was all, 'Tell me where Stacey Branch is right now. I will not ask again.'"

"Oh, wow."

"Yeah, something about it scared me." Elinor grasped her hand. "We're not trying to be cruel, Stacey. It's the opposite. We don't want anything to happen to you."

"You don't have to worry about me, Ellie," Stacey patted the woman's hand affectionately. "I promise I'll be careful."

There was a tap on the door and Bernie, the front desk receptionist, poked his head in. "Hey, Stacey. There's a woman here to see you."

"I wasn't expecting anyone. Who is it?"

"She said her name's Marjorie Swanson."

Stacey's mouth momentarily dropped. "Oh, okay. I guess show her to the conference room. I'll be there in a minute."

Bernie nodded and closed the door.

"Marjorie Swanson," Elinor mused. "Why does that name sound familiar?"

"She owns the Seaside Motel."

"But she hasn't lived here for years."

"I know. I needed some information about an employee. I reached out to her through email. She responded saying she'd be willing to talk to me, but I assumed it would be on the phone or through email. I wonder why she came all the way out."

She grabbed a couple of bottled waters from the fridge in the corner and made her way down the hall to the conference room.

The woman seated at the table was different than Stacey expected. She was in her mid-sixties with wavy, silvery hair and bright blue eyes. She smiled brightly when Stacey entered the room.

"Miss Branch?"

Stacey nodded and sat down next to her and extended her hand. "Mrs. Swanson? I have to admit I'm surprised you came here in person. I expected an email."

"Well, you intrigued me. I haven't been asked about the motel in so long. Then, with that car being discovered, I figured it was worth my attention."

"I have to ask." Stacey leaned forward and grinned at the older woman. "Seaside Motel?"

Mrs. Swanson chuckled. "That was my father's doing. He had an ironic sense of humor, God bless his soul."

"I'm wondering, have the police reached out to you regarding this?"

Mrs. Swanson shook her head. "No. Not since the car was found. A couple of detectives did come out years ago about that woman you wrote about."

Stacey bit her lip. Had Easton lied to her? Were they really investigating if no one even reached out to Marjorie?

"How extensive was the investigation back then?"

"Umm. I'm not sure about the scope of the investigation, but hardly anything happened at the motel. I did receive a call from the Logan's Ridge PD that they were called out to check out a distress call. They didn't find anyone when they came and then the detectives from Boston came out to talk to me. They asked to see the registration book and asked questions about that woman. I couldn't answer because I wasn't there while she was a guest."

"So, were you off that night or already living out of town?"

"I was already living out of town. Business had slowed way down so I moved to be closer to my daughter. I was available if the employees needed anything, but I typically only came out once a month."

"How many employees did you have at the time?"

"Technically three. But a fourth was kind of per diem. Sherry Randall was the night clerk and the manager, then there was the day clerk, Carol Jacobs. Cindy was our housekeeper. But since we weren't getting much business, I cut her down to twice a week for dusting and changing the bedding."

"And the per diem?"

"Marty Randall. He wasn't on the payroll, but he was good at fixing things so he would fix things as needed in exchange for him and Sherry staying on site."

"Marty and Sherry lived at the motel?" Somehow, that escaped her. "Why?"

"Well, Marty wasn't the most pleasant man," Marjorie sighed. "He didn't get along with people and he had a record. They were having a hard time finding somewhere to stay."

Stacey cocked her head to the side. "But I was told he worked at Jimmy Alderman's."

"He did. He serviced the cars if I'm remembering right. He had a habit of offending customers, so Jimmy only had him come in after closing. With such limited hours, he didn't make a lot. It was a good arrangement. The motel had all these empty rooms, one of which was the size of a small apartment, and I got free repairs. We were able to help each other out."

"So, you said Sherry was the night clerk. I'm guessing she was the one to check Susanna in?"

Marjorie nodded. "Yes. It would have been her. According to the records, Susanna checked in in the middle of the night."

"But she didn't say anything about it?"

"No. But that wasn't unusual. By that point in time, we rarely got customers. I was only brought into it if there was a problem."

"So, the day of Susanna's phone call," Stacey flipped back through her notes, "that was during the day, wasn't it?"

"It was."

"So, where was Carol? Your day clerk?"

"Some sort of scheduling mix-up. Carol said Sherry told her the motel would be closed that day because an electrician was coming out and would need to cut the power. That was scheduled for the following week. I assumed communication broke down."

"You closed down not long after this, though."

"Yes. Sherry quit. With customers being so rare, it didn't seem worth it to hire a replacement."

"Did she say why she quit?"

"She said her sister died, and they were moving to California to take care of her kids."

"She couldn't bring the kids here?"

"She said they didn't want to take the kids away from their environment and they could stay in her sister's house. It seemed reasonable enough."

"Did you ever have any issues with Sherry?"

"No, she was the sweetest. A hard worker, personable, everyone liked her. We never understood what she was doing with a prick like Marty."

"Where on site did they live?"

"Room fourteen. It was the only one with a kitchenette."

"Do you mind if I see that unit?"

"Why?"

"Well, I'll be straight with you. Sherry and Marty's names keep popping up. Tony Bradford saw Susanna broken down on the side of the road that night and said Marty helped her. Then she comes to the motel. They left abruptly right after this, and I haven't been able to find anything on them after. It's like they dropped off the face of the planet."

"Wouldn't that mean they didn't get in trouble?" Marjorie asked. "Are you able to see more than newspaper articles?"

"I can't see everything the police can, but I can see a bit more than that. I should have at the least been able to come up with an address. There's nothing. Did she leave any forwarding information?"

Marjorie shook her head. "No. I'm more than happy to go over to the motel with you and see if they left anything in their old unit. I doubt we'll find anything useful after all this time, though."

Fifteen minutes later, Marjorie unlocked the door for unit fourteen and stepped aside for Stacey to go inside. Stacey hadn't told Marjorie she was going to investigate this room one way or another, but her cooperation made things easier.

The unit was covered in cobwebs and dust, as neglected as room one was. It was a similar floor plan that extended back. A small kitchen counter, stove, and fridge was directly next to the dresser with the old TV on it and behind that was a table and chairs.

Stacey opened drawers and searched them. To her surprise, Marjorie did the same. The dresser was empty, as was the closet.

There were still dishes in the cabinets but nothing other than that. She was about to give up when Marjorie called out to her.

Stacey glanced back from where her place near the bathroom when she heard a loud bang. Marjorie tried to push a drawer in, but it wouldn't slide in.

"Something's jammed back there," Marjorie said more to herself than Stacey and yanked the drawer all the way out. A yellowed envelope was taped to the underside and crumpled on the edge.

Stacey ran over and ripped the envelope from the drawer and opened it. It was a letter that read:

Dear Sherry,

I worry about you. Your last letter was troubling. I can't believe Marty blamed you for the miscarriage when he should have been supporting you. He doesn't deserve you, sister. I know Mom and Dad left me the house, but I am going to leave it for you to have when you leave Marty. I don't need the money, but you do need out of that marriage.

I understand losing a child is never easy and you are probably both on edge, but there is no excuse for him to say and do the things he does. It's not the first time he's treated you poorly. Please consider what I'm saying. If you need money, I will send you money. GET OUT of there. PLEASE.

Lots of love,

Your sister,

Priscilla

Jackpot. Another way to find Sherry. "Priscilla? Is this the sister that died?"

"She never mentioned a name. She always said, 'my sister this, and my sister that.'"

Stacey picked the envelope back up to study it more closely. There was a California address on it. "Well, I'll be able to find out with this."

Chapter Eleven

Stacey sighed and sat back from her computer to rub her eyes.

"You alright, chick?" Elinor asked, stopping beside her desk.

Stacey nodded and gave Elinor a quick rundown of her meeting with Marjorie Swanson and their later search of room fourteen.

"I'm not sure if it's a dead end or not," she admitted. "I checked out the address on the envelope and it was, in fact, owned by a Priscilla Riley back in '96. She also owned another home, which I'm guessing is the one referenced in the letter. However, she died in '98, and her home was sold. That same year there was a fire at the other home. It wasn't salvaged."

Elinor sat on the edge of the desk and narrowed her eyes. "So, you think Sherry and Marty were living in the additional home?"

"Well, that's what the letter seemed to indicate. Priscilla wanted Sherry to have the house but for when she left Marty. Who's to know if she would have allowed him to live there as well? Also, we know Sherry lied about why they were leaving."

"No other siblings?"

Stacey shook her head. "Nope. In fact, the girls weren't even related by blood."

"What?"

Stacey turned back to her computer screen to read off the information. "Priscilla's father and Sherry's mother got married when the girls were toddlers and were together until her death. He died six months after. The girls were raised together and considered each other sisters."

Elinor narrowed her eyes and studied Stacey carefully. "I know what you're thinking."

Stacey deliberately stared over her shoulder and fixated on a spot on the wall. "No, you don't."

"You're thinking they killed Susanna and took off with those kids."

"Okay, maybe you know what I'm thinking."

"Stacey," Elinor shook her head. "I'm not disagreeing with you. Why else would they disappear right after she goes missing and lie about why they're leaving?"

"Not to mention Priscilla didn't have any kids."

"How is that relevant?"

"Sherry told people she moved to take custody of her sister's kids."

"I forgot about that. So, why are you debating about Priscilla being a dead end?"

"Well, if my theory is right, they were in California. I'm trying to decide if I should go out there. Sure, Priscilla is gone but her husband is still alive. Someone may have known them. There might be a lead."

"But after twenty-six years, there could be nothing."

Stacey shot a finger pistol. "Exactly."

Her cell phone beeped, and she checked the message on the screen before turning to shut off her computer.

"Who's that?" Elinor asked.

"I'm not at liberty to say," Stacey told her without looking up.

"Theo with the lab?"

"Yep."

"Gotcha." With that, Elinor moved toward her desk but Stacey called out to stop her. "Do you have any plans tonight?"

"No, why? What's up?

"I need to go to Abington. Everyone's so antsy about me going anywhere alone. I might get less heat if you come with me."

"What's in Abington?"

"Maybe nothing," Stacey admitted. "Apparently, when Susanna would drive from Boston to Georgia, she took scheduled stops. Always at the same places. The hotel she normally stayed at halfway was closed the week she went missing. Her sister thinks she would have pressed through to her next stop in Abington. I was gonna go over there and see if she ever made it there. I'm hoping to find something that might tell me how she ended up in DeSoto."

"So, recreate the scene?"

"Basically. Yeah."

"Damn," Elinor shook her head with a wicked smile. "You should have become a crime scene investigator instead of a reporter."

"Too messy."

"Yeah. I'll go with you, chick."

"Cool. Until then," she grinned. "Duty calls."

When Stacey rang the bell at the lab, Theo popped his head around the corner of a doorframe before entering and approaching with a big grin on his face.

"Someone is a busy little bee," he told her.

She smiled. She'd overnighted him the hair samples she'd gotten from David Patterson's house before leaving for Georgia. "So, what's the word?"

"Well, let's start from the beginning," he said as he typed a few keys on his keyboard to bring up a report. "The stain from the motel is positive for blood. I cross-referenced that with the hair sample you sent and got a match for Susanna Patterson."

Stacey thought about what David said about his phone conversation with Susanna. *I told her to hide.* Did she hide in the closet? What happened to her after? She nodded for him to continue.

"There was also a stray hair on that blanket that was a match to Bethany."

That wasn't too surprising considering David identified the stuffed dog as Bethany's. "Alright, well, thanks. I'll let you know if anything else pops up."

She turned to leave but stopped when she saw his face. "Why do you have a shit-eating grin?"

"That's not even the best part," he practically bounced with excitement.

"That's all I submitted to you."

"Yeah, but I did you a solid," he said, grabbing her arm and pulling her through a door behind the desk.

"Theo!" she protested. "I'm not supposed to be back here!"

"I brought you here for scheduled maintenance on the system. The cameras will be down for a few minutes, so we have to be quick."

He led her down a corridor into a large room she recognized to be a giant garage. Parked on the far side was Susanna's car.

"Oh my God!" She ran up to get a close-up view. "What's it doing here?"

"Police brought it in for evaluation," he said, his voice bouncing with pride. "Don't touch it."

Stacey checked the windows. The backseat still held two car seats. There were no noticeable stains.

"Okay, come on, come on, come on," Theo tugged her elbow, pulling her along to the back of the car.

The trunk was unlatched and there was a jagged hole in the back of it. "What? Isn't that where the license plate goes?"

"Yep," he grinned at her expectantly with gleaming eyes.

"Okay, I'm lost."

"This particular model didn't have the safety latch built on the inside. But—" he pointed toward the keyhole. "The lock was busted. There are marks here to show force was used to break through this hole, knocking off the license plate."

Stacey's heartrate increased, and she watched as he opened the trunk further with a gloved hand. Inside was a smattering of soaked bags and a length of frayed rope.

"Oh my God," she whispered as the realization hit her. "She was in the trunk."

"This keeps getting wilder," Elinor shook her head. "You get all these exciting things pushing your case forward. It's like something from a movie."

"Well, I don't know if I'd call it exciting," Stacey smiled warmly.

"Well, I mean it's dark, sure. Don't get me wrong," Elinor stumbled. "But I write obituaries. Any twists on my articles will trigger heart attacks."

Stacey laughed. "Well, according to Theo, they are dredging the lake tomorrow morning."

"And I bet you'll be there, huh?"

"Front and center."

Stacey checked at her GPS. "It should be coming up on the right."

She slowed her speed slightly, and both women scanned the road.

"I think that's it," Elinor said, pointing to a tall building in the distance.

A quick internet search awarded them with a pancake house and hotel opposite each other on the route Susanna normally drove, like Mallory said.

Stacey swung the car into the parking lot and Elinor whistled. The building was grand in stature, with huge windows and a circular drive.

"Fancy pants," she said her breath.

They got out of the car and went inside, where they were met with a bored clerk, who was reading a magazine and chewing gum.

"Hi," Stacey said. "This may be a long shot, but I'm investigating a missing person's case. A person of interest was supposed to stay at your establishment, and I was hoping you could tell me if she ever checked in? It would have been in the '90s."

"Our computer records don't go back that far," the clerk rolled her eyes. "But files are kept in the basement going back to the 60s. Come back in the morning, and the owner might check."

"You can't check?"

"No," the girl huffed. "I can't leave my post. I'm the only one on duty."

Without another word, the girl stuck ear buds deliberately into her ears, indicating she was done with the conversation.

Stacey grunted in frustration and stepped away from the desk. "I thought fancy places like this had better customer service," she hissed to Elinor through clenched teeth.

"We're not technically customers," Elinor whispered back, but she jerked her head in the opposite direction.

Stacey followed her gaze to a door that said, *Stairwell*.

They glanced back over at the clerk who bopped her head to the music thundering in her ears, and flipped through her magazine, oblivious to their presence.

They casually walked to the door and walked through it undetected. "God, that girl is bad at her job," Stacey murmured.

"Maybe, but at least we know where to go."

They followed the stairs down and walked through a single door leading to a room filled to the brim with shelves of file boxes.

"Alright," Stacey said. "Fan out."

They went to opposite sides of the room and made their way down the rows of files, carefully scanning dates on the front of each box.

Stacey's pulse quickened when she got to a row from the 90s and sped up until she found 1996. The third box held records from the time of Susanna's disappearance. She opened it up and flipped through the papers. Going through the date of her disappearance three times before she was satisfied.

"Ellie!" Stacey called out.

Footsteps headed her way, and Elinor quickly rounded the corner to see. "Did you find something?"

"Susanna didn't make it here."

"Well, shit," Elinor sighed and put her hands on her hips. "What now?"

When the women made it back to the car, Stacey spoke up again for the first time. "Okay. You're driving from Boston to Georgia. Your preferred hotel is closed. This is your next stop, only you never make it. How do you end up in DeSoto?"

Elionor chewed her lip. "Well, I'd be tired. It's late at night too. I don't get it."

Let your gift in, a soft voice thundered inside her head. She wasn't sure where it came from, but she chose to listen.

She closed her eyes tightly and gripped the steering wheel with all her might.

The night seemed to turn and swirl all around her. She saw Susanna blinking furiously, as she took her exit. Then, shortly after the exit, she'd followed a large detour sign due to a collision.

Stacey's eyes snapped back open, and she took short, precise breaths to try to calm her thundering heart.

"Stace, you okay?" Elinor asked.

"She exited too early," Stacey ignored her question. She needed to get out what she'd seen in case she forgot it. "She exited early to detour around a wreck and got lost."

"How could you possibly know that?" Elinor wondered.

"I don't know. But I'm positive that's what happened. I'll prove it tomorrow."

With that, she started the ignition and threw the car into reverse.

CHAPTER TWELVE

Stacey stood behind the crime scene tape the next morning next to the lake. Now the police were there with a forensics team dredging the lake in search of a body.

They'd been searching for hours, and she was almost ready to give up when they emerged in their scuba gear. The chief approached the team lead, and Stacey positioned herself to better hear.

"Nothing down there."

"You're absolutely sure?"

"We checked it twice."

He nodded. "Well, we needed to be sure. It looks like she managed to break out. Question is how she ended up there in the first place."

The chief went to move away before he spotted her at the tree line and strode up to her. "Miss Branch."

"Chief."

He sighed. "I'm assuming you overheard that conversation?"

"That Susanna Patterson was in the trunk and broke out? Yeah, I heard that."

He sneered. "Why don't you go be a nuisance to someone else?"

"The community has a right to be informed," she said coolly. "I don't intend on covering up this case a second time."

"It wasn't covered up," he said through gritted teeth. "We operated on the information we had at the time."

"So, the FBI were never involved?"

"That would have been up to Boston to initiate."

"So, then you're investigating Marty and Sherry Randall?"

"How the hell do you know about them?"

"I pay attention."

"Fine. Yes. Sherry was the last person known to have seen them, so, naturally, we'll need to speak to her."

"Hmm," Stacey said in a placating tone and smiled at the chief.

"You need to hold off on putting anything in print."

"You need to be reasonable."

"Look. I'm holding a press conference in two hours to make an open statement that we're reopening the case. Can you wait that long?"

"That I can do."

He walked off without saying another word, shaking his head vigorously.

Easton then stepped up, "So, the chief told you."

"Don't play stupid. You were standing right over there. You heard us."

"Okay." He hooked his thumbs in his front pockets and stared down at the ground.

"So, you guys let my brother out of jail yet?"

"He was only there for questioning. We let him go for now. He is still a person of interest."

"Gavin couldn't hurt a fly."

"According to his record, he could."

"What? That stint in juvie? He took a joy ride."

"Sounds like you only have half of the story."

She narrowed her eyes and jabbed her finger into his chest. "Listen here, Buster. Are you trying to tell me you know more about my family than I do?"

"I'm telling you I've seen the reports. Plus, it's standard to investigate the spouse first. When you figure that in with her phone being at his job—"

"There're a hundred different reasons her phone could have been there. It doesn't mean anything. He has an alibi. He spent the night at my parents' because I was out of town."

Easton tilted his head to the side. "Wow."

"Wow, what?"

"Your parents said he left at ten the night before."

Ice rolled through her veins, and she stared at him in disbelief.

"My God," he said, his voice gentler now. "You really didn't know, did you?"

Stacey couldn't do anything but stare at her plate and absently push the food around with her fork at lunch. She couldn't stop thinking about her conversation with Easton.

"Stacey? Are you okay, honey?" Alice asked her as she grasped her hand.

"Hmm?" Stacey snapped out of it and realized her mother was talking to her. "I'm okay. Sorry, Mom."

The two women were having a rare lunch alone as Paul had taken the opportunity to run into town and grab some supplies he needed.

"Mom?"

"What is it, honey?"

"Why was Gavin in juvie?"

"You know the answer to that, dear. He took your daddy's truck for a spin without permission."

"Was that all that happened?"

Alice narrowed calculating eyes. "Why on Earth are you asking about that after all this time?"

"Because Easton let slip today that one of the reasons they are investigating him so closely in Angie's disappearance is due to his record. Something tells me a spin with a truck as a teenager wouldn't have that kind of result."

Alice pointed a finger at her and switched her tone to the harshest Stacey ever heard it. "You are not going to write a story about your brother, young lady."

"Of course not. What do you take me for? I want to know the truth so I can help him."

Alice sighed and lowered her finger. "Well, I guess it won't do no harm in telling you now. You were so young at the time, and we all agreed it was best you not know everything."

"So, tell me now."

"He did take a ride in your daddy's truck. That part was true. But what we didn't tell you is he picked up a girl to have one of them midnight dates. She wasn't supposed to be out either. Well, they went parking and he got forceful."

Stacey's jaw dropped. "You mean?"

Alice inclined her head. "She managed to get out of the truck and run away, but she was real busted up and had to go to the hospital. When her daddy showed up over here, naturally we were horrified. We took him straight to that center."

Stacey leaned her elbows on the table and rested her head in her hands. It was a lot to absorb. Gavin was the nicest, most considerate man she knew. Something didn't add up.

"Now, we love your brother. We in no way believe he's a bad person. Hormones are running rampant at that age, especially in boys. But he had to be taught that kind of behavior was not acceptable."

"Okay," Stacey hesitated and lifted her head back up. "But do you think that had anything to do with Angie going missing?"

"I don't want to believe that. He has toed the line since that unfortunate incident. 'Far as I know, he hasn't even had a traffic ticket. But he did lie to the police about where he was, and we were not going to back up that kind of lie."

"Okay." Stacey whispered. "Okay."

"I personally believe his lie was about something else entirely. That Angie is no good. Her background—she probably left."

"Her background? She was an abandoned child. How was that her fault?"

"I don't mean to say it's her fault," Alice protested. "It isn't. She doesn't know any different. She can't help it. But it is likely she couldn't take the pressure. Knowing you'll never measure up can't be easy."

"Wow," Stacey bit down the urge to scream. "That's the first stupid thing I've ever heard you say."

Alice's mouth dropped open, and Stacey rose from her seat. She made haste to the second floor and the solitude of her bedroom.

Once the bedroom door was closed tightly behind her, Stacey covered her mouth with her hand and sank onto the bed. Someone was lying to her, and she had no idea who it was. She grabbed a pillow and pulled it to her chest as she allowed the thoughts to roll wildly through her mind.

The police investigating Gavin so hard indicated he did have something in his past to hide, but Stacey had never known him to be a violent person. Even when they were kids, and he teased her mercilessly, he'd never caused her any kind of physical pain. Not even so much as a thrown toy in a tantrum.

Stacey needed someone to talk to who wouldn't judge her. Someone who would just let her talk about the way she felt. She thought of her childhood friend, Beth again. Beth had been on her mind a lot lately.

The pair had always talked about the tough stuff without judgement. If Beth were here, she wouldn't be calling Gavin a creep, or Stacey naïve. She'd just be there.

As Stacey laid down, she wished they'd never lost contact.

CHAPTER THIRTEEN

"What are you doing here?" Easton snapped when he opened the door to his apartment.

"I need to talk to you."

He stuck his head out the door and quickly glanced each way before taking her elbow and steering her inside. "You shouldn't be here."

He didn't insist she leave. He offered her a beverage and returned to the living room a moment later to hand her a bottle of water.

"What's up, Stacey?"

"I talked to my mom about Gavin."

"What did she tell you?"

"She told me about the girl."

"I'm sorry."

She believed him. He wasn't exhibiting any of his usual cockiness. He seemed truly sympathetic.

"I didn't mean for you to find out that way," he told her. "I thought you knew."

"Do you know who it was?"

He shook his head. "She was a minor, so her name was redacted from the record, and it was before my time."

Stacey inclined her head, a million thoughts swirling through her mind all at once.

"What are you thinking?" he asked her gently.

"It doesn't make sense," she shook her head. "It's not like Gavin at all. He's a teddy bear. He's so respectful."

"I know it's hard, but you have to remember most people don't want to believe their loved ones are capable of such things."

"It's more than that," she objected. "He's so respectful of women. I remember when I was in high school, a boy smacked my ass, and Gavin put him right up against the lockers and asked him what made him think it was okay to put his hands on anyone without their consent."

"You're his sister. Some guys are hypocrites about that."

"And" Stacey continued as though he hadn't spoken, "Angie confided in me he didn't even kiss her until they'd dated like a month. Even though she sent him all kinds of signs."

Easton looked at her sympathetically. "I can't do anything about something that happened fifteen years ago, Stacey."

"I know that, and I don't expect you to," she said as she grabbed his hand and gave it a desperate squeeze. "But please don't hold it against him now. Don't punish him for something that's basically my fault."

"Your fault?"

She downcast her eyes. "I don't have any proof, but I can't shake this gut feeling she was taken as revenge for my story."

"I thought you were convinced she was grabbed by the same person that took those other girls."

"I did at first," she admitted, "but I keep learning more and more and that theory doesn't make sense anymore.'

Easton leaned back in his seat and nodded for her to continue.

"It feels so similar to Susanna Patterson to me. Plus, it happens right after my story comes out."

"Other than it being a woman, what makes you think this is anything like Susanna Patterson's case?"

"Well, she'd found out she was pregnant. So, she technically has a child with her. Plus, there was the phone call he got. It makes me think about the phone call David Patterson received from Susanna. The last time anyone heard from her."

"Gavin didn't say anything about her being pregnant."

She nodded. "He's not exactly excited. He's afraid he'll be like our dad, and he doesn't want that kind of relationship with his children. My parents found out the night before. There was a big fight with them because they don't like her and don't want them having children together. That's why he spent the night there. Angie told him not to come home."

"Except he didn't spend the night there."

"How do we know that?"

Easton narrowed his eyes. "Stacey, do you realize what you're saying? Someone is lying. If it's not Gavin, it's your parents. Why would they lie about something like that?"

"I don't know! I don't know!" she exclaimed and ran a nervous hand through her hair. "Maybe because they don't like her? They don't want them together."

"So badly they'd risk their son going to prison for a crime he didn't commit?"

Tears pooled in her eyes, and he patted her hand. "I'm not trying to be an ass. Really, I'm not. It's that there are a lot of holes in that theory."

She nodded. "I don't know what you could do about it, I thought I should tell you. I also wanted to ask you a favor."

"What's that?"

"I'm going to California for a couple of days. I was hoping you could check on my parents while I'm gone. I don't want to ask Gavin right now. He probably doesn't want to see them."

Easton's lips tightened as he stared at her for a good thirty seconds before answering her. "Why are you going to California?"

She pulled in a deep breath. "I'm going to visit Jerry Riley."

"You're what?" His tone was sharp and calculated.

So, he was investigating. How did you like that?

"I'm going to see Jerry Riley. Sherry Randall's brother-in-law."

"I know who he is. The question is, how do you know who he is?"

"I told you before. I pay attention."

"Stacey, you can't go there."

"I don't see why not."

"You need to let the police investigate this."

"They haven't been doing a good job so far."

He scowled at her.

"I'm not trying to be a bitch," she said as she threw up her hands. "But it is a fact. I'm glad it's being investigated now, but I can't help but be skeptical over all the things that have been missed."

"What the hell is the point of going to see Jerry?"

"Priscilla owned two houses."

"I *know* that!"

"Did you know one of them was promised to Sherry?"

His eyes widened, and his mouth dropped open.

"You're welcome," she said sarcastically.

"Are you saying she was living there?"

"I don't know, but I intend to find out. She did tell people they were going to California, so I'd say there's a good chance."

"You shouldn't go out there."

"I have to. I'm starting to think they snatched those kids and took off."

He frowned.

"Do you disagree?"

"I can't confirm or deny."

"You agree."

"It doesn't matter if I agree or not. The fact is, if it is true, you could be putting yourself in a hell of a lot of danger."

"I'm going."

"Then I'm going with you."

"But my parents—"
"Don't worry. I'll send Mom over there."

True to his word, Easton called his mother to go and sit with Stacey's parents, packed a bag, and the pair of them headed straight for the airport.

He returned to their seats at the gate and offered her a fast-food bag before sinking down into the chair and stuffing fries in his mouth.

"If anyone asks, I'm not with the police department," he told her as he took a sip of his own drink.

"Why?"

"I didn't exactly go through the proper channels."

She glanced down at her carry-on bag for a moment and bit her lip before speaking. "Then why are you coming with me?"

"I'm not an idiot. Even though you think I am," he stared her dead in the face. "I know you only went out with me that one time to get your mother to shut up. I know you barely tolerate me on a good day. You don't have to believe me here. You probably won't. Despite all that, I consider you a friend. I like you. I respect you so much for putting up with everything you have in your life. I wouldn't have been able to tolerate your family's bullshit if it was me. I don't like you going out here, but I know damn well you're going to do it no matter what anyone says. I might as well make sure you're safe."

She was about to reply when they were called to board.

CHAPTER FOURTEEN

"Are you sure this is it?" Easton asked as he pulled the rental car up in front of the address Stacey had plugged into the GPS.

She checked the address again. "That's what the property records say." They both stared at the empty expanse of green lawn they were parked in front of.

They'd decided to visit the second home in Priscilla's name first on the off chance they might spot Marty or Sherry.

There was an old man working in the garden of the house next door, and Stacey was out of the car approaching him before Easton could blink. He quickly recovered and darted behind her.

"Excuse me!" Stacey said cheerfully as she walked up to the old man.

He sat back from his azaleas and stared up at her from under a wide-brimmed hat. "Yes?"

She extended her hand. "Hi there! Have you lived here long?"

"About thirty years," the man eyed her suspiciously. "Who's asking?"

"I'm so sorry. Where are my manners?" she placed a hand to her chest in mock embarrassment. "I'm Lydia and this is my fiancé, Daniel."

Fiancé? Easton cocked an amused eyebrow. What was her angle here?

"We're looking for my aunt and uncle to invite them to the wedding. The number we have for them is no good, and our letters haven't been answered." She jerked her head toward the empty land and set her hands on her hips. "Of course, now I see why. We came out here in person because it's the last known address we have for them."

The old man brushed the dirt off his hands and got to his feet. "Well, congratulations." His disposition was sunnier already and he smiled at the pair of them. "Your aunt and uncle Martin and Sharon Petersen?"

Stacey and Easton exchanged a look and then Stacey nodded to the man with a big smile. "They sure are. Uncle Marty and Aunt Sherry. Haven't seen them in so long."

The man gestured over his shoulder toward the front door. "Come on in the house. We'll have a chat."

They followed him into the house and down a long hallway toward the kitchen. He pulled down three elegant glasses and poured lemonade from a pitcher.

"I'm surprised you don't already know about what happened," the man told them when they'd settled onto barstools at the kitchen island.

"Well, they really are homebodies," Stacey said knowingly. "They've always liked keeping to themselves. In fact, my mama told me not to expect an answer to our invitation at all. But family's family, and I wanted to make sure they knew so they could make an informed decision."

The man nodded. "That's real considerate of you. Especially in this day and age when all you young folk communicate through text message, email, and the Tok-tok. It would be easy for them to slip through the cracks."

"So, do you know what happened to the house?" Stacey asked as she lifted her glass up to her lips.

"I'm sorry to tell you it burned back in '98."

"Oh my!" She widened her eyes. "Was anyone else living here? Did they have roommates?"

"No, just the family."

"Family?"

"My dear. You don't know about your cousins?" He reached out and patted her hand affectionately. "They had two children. A boy and a girl."

"No, I didn't know." Stacey grasped Easton's hand. "Did you hear that, honey? I have cousins out there somewhere."

The man nodded. "They were a real nice family. Very polite, well-mannered children. Sharon would bring us cookies and cakes when she baked. Didn't talk to Martin as much, but he seemed nice enough. They lived there for a couple of years before the fire. It started on a still night, thank goodness, so none of the surrounding homes were in danger. But that house burned to a crisp. No one was inside it, but arson was suspected."

"How come?" Easton chimed in for the first time.

"Some sort of accelerant was used. A buddy of mine who worked in the fire department at the time told me. Since no one was home and it was the middle of the night, it was suspected they started it themselves. Not that I believed that." the man gave Stacey a lopsided smile. "I couldn't believe anything like that of them. They were such nice people. No. I always figured they were away on vacation or visiting family and got lucky they weren't there."

"Did anything strange happen leading up to that?" Stacey asked. "People hanging around you didn't recognize? Anyone that might have a grudge against them?"

"Well, there was that one man."

"What man?" Easton asked.

"Said he was a police officer. I saw him go over there a couple of times. Then he came over here and offered me money to spy and call him if Martin did anything suspicious. Gave me a business card and everything. He was acting off his rocker. Never thought about it, but I guess that was about a week before the fire."

"I know it's a long shot, but do you still have the card?"

The man shook his head. "Sure don't. I threw it straight in the trashcan as soon as he left. Like I said, he didn't seem like he was working with a full deck of cards, if you know what I mean. But his name was strange. I remember thinking it sounded like he was a character in one of them road rage movies. Like rush hour traffic is what it made me think of."

"Well, thank you," Easton said, swallowing the last of his lemonade and rising to his feet. "It was so nice of you to offer us refreshments and let us know. We have one more place to check before we have to head to the airport. It was nice meeting you."

They both shook hands with the man, and Stacey hissed at Easton as they were walking down the sidewalk toward their rental car. "Why'd you rush us out of there so fast?"

"Henry Rusher was the lead investigator on the Patterson case," he told her in a quiet tone. "I smell a rat."

Two hours later, they were holed up in Stacey's hotel room on their laptops trying to make some sense of what they'd learned.

"Yep. That's what I thought," Easton said as he sat back and tilted his screen for Stacey to see. "Henry Rusher retired two weeks after the house fire."

"There's got to be something we're missing," Stacey said as she studied the screen. "It says here he officially closed the case the same week he retired."

"I can't put my finger on it, but something is off here." Easton shook his head. "Nothing was actively done on the Patterson case after '96. Hell, we didn't even know the case was 'closed.' He conveniently closes the case when he retires? And goes to where Marty and Sherry were?"

"They disappear after he visits too. Not before." Stacey bit her lip. "Easton, do you think he knew where they were all along?"

He shook his head. "He had the resources, but the case wasn't being investigated. No reason to believe he knew all along. More like he didn't try. It doesn't make sense."

They were interrupted by a sharp, authoritative knock on the door. Easton rose from his seat to answer it.

When the elderly man walked in the room, he stepped back from Easton, as if surprised to see him, and then darted his eyes over to Stacey who sat at the table.

"May I help you?" she asked shrewdly.

He didn't answer her. Instead, he began questioning her. "Stacey Branch, I presume?"

"That depends on who's asking."

"Your article made for interesting reading." The man strode over to the table and took the seat opposite her.

"Excuse me," she replied sharply. "Who do you think you are to waltz into my hotel room and welcome yourself to sit without even telling me who the hell you are?"

"Forgive me," he said and extended a hand. "I'm Detective Henry Rusher. I believe it was your handiwork that reopened one of my cases."

"Actually, the car being pulled from the lake reopened the case. Stacey beat the police department to print," Easton said as he strode forward.

"Who are you?" Rusher asked, sneering up at him.

"I'm Easton Gates. I'm with the Logan's Ridge Police Department."

"Then you should know," Rusher said as he shook a finger at him, "better than to be fraternizing with the press, Officer."

"I accompanied Miss Branch for her own protection. You see, her article has caused some less than desirable attention."

"Hmm," Rusher turned back toward Stacey. "Well, that happens when you mess around with things you don't understand."

"All I did was report on the news." Stacey closed her laptop and leaned forward on her elbows. "The rest sort of fell into place. You know, it's funny how one little newspaper article can have all this evidence coming out of the woodwork when police seemingly couldn't find a shred of evidence."

Rusher's eyes flashed. "That's because there was none."

"Really?" she raised an eyebrow at him. "I spoke to the same witnesses. Only I followed up on what I was told. I found plenty of evidence."

"The car? You'll have to forgive the officers for not thinking about checking underwater. Besides, that doesn't prove anything, anyway. She could've driven it into the lake before starting her new life. It doesn't invalidate the original ruling."

"Maybe not by itself," Stacey agreed. "But her blood being found at the motel, and Marty and Sherry Randall moving across the country, changing their names, and suddenly having two children might spark a little interest. Especially when it comes out that the lead investigator knew and didn't put it in any reports."

Rusher slammed his hand down on the table. "You listen here—"

"No, you listen," she growled in a tone that shut him up and dropped his jaw. "I might not know why you didn't put Marty and Sherry's locations in any other reports, but I am damn sure going to find out. Maybe you wanted a clean record for your retirement and were too lazy to put in the work to save this family. Who knows? The fact of the matter is no one likes a dirty cop. And what you have done screams cover up."

"You don't want to screw with me," he hissed.

"Maybe you don't want to screw with me," she told him flatly before rising from her seat and striding to the door. "Now kindly get the hell out."

He thundered toward the door. "This isn't over," he spat before storming into the hall.

"Yeah, yeah. Tough guy." She slammed the door behind him.

Easton stood in the corner with his arms crossed in front of his chest and an amused twinkle in his eyes. "Damn, Branch. I didn't know you had it in you."

"Yeah, I'm a total badass," she said with disinterest and picked up her purse. "Let's go. I'm hungry."

CHAPTER FIFTEEN

They chose a steakhouse on the edge of town and were more than ready to sink into the free bread on the table the moment they were in their seats.

"The nerve of that guy," Stacey exclaimed as she tore a roll with her teeth. "And you. So much for being my protecter."

"You seemed like you had things under control," he chuckled as he studied the menu. "You literally had him speechless."

"Well, I have a lot of practice with obstinate pricks."

"Ouch," he placed his hands over his heart as if she'd shot him.

She smiled. "Maybe that came out wrong. I mean, I'm used to strong male energy in my life. I've needed to be tough to survive."

"Your dad?"

"My dad, Gavin, you," she sighed. "My best friend's dad growing up was a mean drunk. The things that man would say and do to Beth—it's hard to believe anyone could be that heartless to their own child. Poor girl was a bundle of nerves for years. She ran off and got married to escape him. I honestly don't think she even loved the man she married, but he was her ticket out. Eventually, you have to build up big, strong walls and give these big, strong men the same energy back. Otherwise, they think they own you."

"Well, you definitely ripped Rusher's balls off and stuffed them down his throat."

A woman at the next table slapped her table, making the dinnerware clank, and narrowed her eyes at him.

"How you doing?" he asked her with a big smile.

The woman rolled her eyes and turned back to her plate.

Stacey giggled and raised a fist to her mouth to disguise the food she hadn't finished chewing.

He shrugged his shoulders. "You get what you get listening to other people's conversations."

They took a brief pause when the waitress came over to take their orders before returning to their conversation.

"So, what happened to your friend?" Easton asked. "I never see you with anyone but your parents or that woman from the newspaper office."

"Elinor," Stacey nodded. "Ellie's great. But no, you're right. I haven't seen Beth in a long time. When she got married, she drove off into the sunset. I got a couple of letters in the beginning but eventually the contact stopped. I was still with my parents a couple of years after that, and communication isn't so easy in their neck of the woods."

"Come on," Easton chuckled in disbelief. "This is the information age. You traced Marty and Sherry Randall across the country, but you can't find your childhood best friend?"

"It's not that I can't," she protested. "It's just so much time has passed. We're not the same people anymore. What could we even talk about?"

"You're high!" he exclaimed. "I haven't seen my best buddy in about ten years either, but we still talk on the phone and text constantly. He's been married for ten years, has three kids, and owns his own business. I'm a thirty-two-year-old single cop with no social life. He loves sports and I couldn't care less. He's a country music guy, and I'm rock all the way. But I know one thing for damn sure. My life is better for him being in it, and I can't imagine cutting him out because time has passed."

"Well, when you put it like that—" Stacey's cheeks flushed in embarrassment.

"What you have to ask yourself is did she feel like family?"

"Yeah, she did."

"Do you feel like your life is missing something without her?"

"Yeah, I do," Stacey admitted.

"Then get your lazy fingers to work and look her up. You might be surprised at what you find."

She studied him for a minute before giving him a smirk. "Damn, Gates. I didn't know you had it in you."

"I hate when I see people throwing away what's good for them."

Easton's phone chirped, and his eyes widened when he saw the message. "You didn't tell your parents you were coming to California?"

"How do you know that?"

"My mom," he waved his phone. "She says your dad has been on a warpath, and your mom's crying. She tried to calm them down by telling them I came with you, but that seemed to upset your dad more. Apparently, I shouldn't have accompanied you. I should have stopped you."

Stacey took his phone and studied the message. "I wonder why this beeped now. Time stamp shows this message was sent several hours ago. It would have been the first shock of me being gone. I'm sure everything's fine now."

"Why didn't you tell them?"

"They made such a big deal when I went to see David Patterson and they were fighting with Gavin. I didn't want to hear it. Fine, I'm an awful daughter."

"You're not an awful daughter. You're suffocated." He reached across the table to take her hand. "I like your parents, but they are a little odd and they treat you like you're still a little girl. It shouldn't be the end of the world because you leave their sight for a few days. That's strange."

"And your mother's not controlling?" Her voice had no malice. She smiled. "I seem to recall an awkward date because *both* our mothers wouldn't shut up."

"That's easy," he grinned. "She wants grandbabies and thinks I'm her last chance. It's normal for mothers with children of a certain age to start pushing them to find someone and settle down. She's pretty chill about everything else."

"You're her last chance? You have siblings."

"Yeah, but Abby can't have kids, and Jeremy can't stay out of trouble. No one wants him to have a baby."

"I'm sorry. I didn't realize." She'd only met Easton's siblings a handful of times. His brother, Jeremy, gave her the creeps.

"He spent most of his teenage years in a juvenile detention center. Then in and out of jail since he's turned eighteen. I don't like labels, but if I had to give him one it would be 'the bad seed.'"

"Well, to hear my parents talk, that's what Gavin is," sadness clouded Stacey's eyes. "But with him, it was only one incident. It was a big deal. I still can't believe he would do that. I need to talk to him about it."

"Teenagers can do stupid things," Easton said gently. "I wouldn't worry about it too much. Like you said, he was straight after."

The waitress came over with their plates. Her cheery demeanor had changed since she'd taken their orders. Her cheeks were puffy, and her eyes red as though she'd been crying. Stacey saw a flash in her mind's eye of the waitress in the break room realizing her wedding ring was gone. She'd torn the room apart and not found it. Then Stacey saw a flash of the ring rolling under a rack in the kitchen.

"Hey," Stacey said in a comforting tone, and she took the girl's hand in both hers, startling her. "Don't worry about your ring. It's in the kitchen. It rolled under the spice rack."

The woman's eyes went wide, and she pulled her hand out of Stacey's grasp and rushed off, glancing over her shoulder at them.

"Umm, you want to explain that?" Easton asked.

Stacey sighed. She didn't normally tell people her secret. She knew it wasn't normal and didn't want to be judged. Easton saw this interaction though, and she had no choice but to tell him.

"I know things sometimes."

"You mean you're psychic?"

"I wouldn't say that." She let out another breath. "I can't tell the future; I don't see ghosts. Mostly I'll know where lost things are and sometimes when emotions are strong, I'll see a situation."

"Is that how you've known things about this case?"

"No," she said adamantly. "I did see a woman and child outside a broken-down car out on Route 6 awhile back. Turned around and they were gone. I do believe now it was Susanna Patterson and her daughter, but I didn't realize that at the time."

Easton's silence spoke volumes.

"Go ahead. Laugh. Make fun of me. Get it over with."

"Why would I do that?"

She narrowed her eyes.

"I've seen you have good instincts. I didn't know where it came from, obviously. It makes sense to me though."

"Usually when people catch me doing it, they act like I'm some sort of freak. They don't want to believe in it because the unknown scares them."

"I believe in it."

Stacey stared hard into his eyes, searching for any sign of deception, but there was none. She saw him, really saw him, for the first time. This was a good man with amazing instincts and a genuine heart. Not a bad body either.

"What?" he asked.

She flushed and studied her plate. "Maybe we should get me drunk."

An hour later, Easton pushed her against the wall outside her hotel room. She fumbled in her purse for her key, and he couldn't keep his hands off her. He nipped at her neck, sending chills racing through her body.

She pushed back suddenly and flipped around to face him. She grabbed him roughly by the face and shoved her lips to his. It felt like his lips were made for hers.

He wasn't gentle as his tongue invaded her mouth. Every part of her ached for him. "Wait, wait," she breathlessly whispered, pulling her head back.

He groaned in protest, causing her to giggle. "The key. We have to find the key. Otherwise, you're going to take me right here in the hallway."

"I don't have a problem with that," he growled.

She laughed again, digging through her purse again. "Pretty sure that's considered public indecency, Officer."

Her fingers tightened around the slim card, and she pulled it from her purse triumphantly. "Got it!"

His hands were all over her as she unlocked the door. As soon as the door slammed shut behind them, she shoved him to the bed.

Stacey was awoken sometime in the middle of the night to the sound of her phone ringing. As soon as her eyes opened, it registered the room was silent. Another vision. She wished she could understand what it meant. Stacey rolled back against the warmth of Easton's chest. She flushed. One-night stands weren't her thing. Especially with Easton Gates. For reasons she couldn't explain, she felt more at ease with him now than she had on their actual date. Her thoughts were interrupted by her cell phone ringing. She reached for it and groaned when she saw she had fifteen missed calls from Gavin.

"Gavin?" she yawned.

"Stacey?" The sound of his voice made her sit straight up in the bed. He sounded panicked, and she could maybe count the number of times he'd been like that on one hand. "Are you okay?"

"I'm fine. What about you? What's wrong?"

"It's Mom and Dad. They've been attacked."

CHAPTER SIXTEEN

Stacey was a nervous wreck until they were finally able to get home. Despite leaving the hotel immediately after Gavin's call, they'd been stuck at the airport for more than twenty-four hours.

They went straight to the hospital from the airport and burst into a room with double beds.

Alice's eyes flashed with anger, and she turned back to the window. Easton's mother, Teresa, sat in a chair next to her bed, holding her hand.

Paul, however, did not turn away. "Do you see what happens when you leave your parents defenseless?" he said in way of greeting.

"Hey now," Easton stepped forward and put a comforting hand on Stacey's shoulder. "This isn't her fault."

"The hell it's not."

"She arranged for someone to sit with you," Easton said staring at his own mother.

Paul snorted. "A lot of good that did."

"Do you not realize," Easton snapped, "whoever did this would have done it regardless of who was there? Stacey being there wouldn't have changed anything."

"Well, if she wasn't messing about with things she had no business being in, people wouldn't be after her family."

"What happened?" Stacey interjected the men's conversation. Arguing wasn't doing anyone any good.

Alice sighed from her bed, but still didn't make eye contact. "I was cleaning up in the kitchen, and I heard the back door open. I thought it was Teresa, so I was chattering away, and I felt something hit me hard in the back of the head. I blacked out."

"I heard a loud noise, so I ran up to the house," Paul said. "I went in through the back door and saw your mother on the floor and a person in black standing over her. They pulled a knife out of her side. I ran forward and tackled them off her. Then they punched me. I tried to get the knife away from them, but I couldn't, so I hit them with the table lamp. I felt my arm snap, and everything went dark."

Easton frowned at his crying mother. "Where were you?"

"I was going to bake a pie for them, but Alice was out of sugar. I made a quick run to the market and went straight back." Her voice cracked on the last word, and her shoulders shook as she told the story. "They were on the floor when I walked in the door. Both of them were unconscious and there was blood everywhere. Twenty minutes. I was only gone twenty minutes."

"So, why didn't you call me?"

"I'm sorry," she snapped out with an icy tone. "I was a little busy calling ambulances and rushing to the hospital."

"Miss Branch?" came the soft voice of a nurse in the corner Stacey hadn't previously noticed. "Your mother lost quite a bit of blood. Would you mind donating?"

"Of course."

"I don't need her blood!" Alice exclaimed. "I've already been getting transfusions. Besides, it's her fault I'm in this situation in the first place."

Stacey stung as if she'd been slapped. Her sweet natured mother never spoke to her like this.

"Mrs. Branch, there's no guarantee you'd receive your daughter's blood. It's customary for family and friends of transfusion patients to give blood." The nurse told her.

"No," Alice hissed. "It's not fair to victims." She shot her gaze over to Stacey. "I want you out of here! Get out! I can't stand the sight of you."

Stacey ran out of the room with tears streaming down her face and, once in the hallway, put her hands up to her face.

Easton followed her into the hall and put a comforting hand on her arm. "Are you okay?"

She nodded. "It's just—I've never seen her like that. Even when Gavin was in trouble. She hates me."

"She doesn't hate you. She's scared."

Stacey shook her head. "Maybe it is my fault."

"No, it's not." She kept shaking her head. "It's not," he said more insistently.

She stopped shaking her head and tears flowed freely.

"You're not going to be able to stay at the farmhouse for a while," he told her gently. "Do you still have your apartment?"

She nodded. "Yeah. God, it's going to be a mess though."

"It's better than nothing." He rubbed her arms. "Come on. Let's go get your things."

Easton

Easton's mind reeled with all the information he'd learned over the past couple of days. He sat at his desk in the police station going over the old files from Henry Rusher, trying to find anything at all that seemed out of place.

Stacey wasn't wrong when she said she smelled a cover up. He'd been thinking the same thing, only she'd beaten him to the punch with confronting the bastard.

Now, he was even more convinced of it as he saw after closing the Patterson case, the man had a perfect record. With the way things appeared now, Easton had to wonder how many of the man's cases were mismanaged or flat out ignored for the sake of good numbers. There was doubt in his mind the case being closed right before he retired was no coincidence.

"Gates," the chief said as he approached his desk.

"Chief. What can I do for you?"

"Have you seen the email I sent you?"

"No."

"Well, I only sent it a couple of minutes ago. Open it up now. You need to see this."

Easton changed tabs to pull up his email and open the last one from the chief. He scanned through the information and a mountain of emotions flooded through him all at once. Confusion, understanding, and finally worry.

"Is this what I think it is?"

"Oh yeah." The chief nodded. "On top of that, the hospital called. Turns out there's been a disturbance."

Dread gripped his belly, and he sprung from his seat, grabbing his keys. "Oh, my God. Stacey."

"Come in!" Stacey called out to him from inside the apartment.

Easton stepped in and saw she was on the phone, so he walked over to an armchair opposite the couch where she sat. She wore a worried expression on her face, and she seemed so tired compared to a few days before.

"Alright. Thanks for letting me know," she said and pinched the bridge of her nose as she hung up.

"Everything okay?" He asked her gently even though he was sure he knew what the phone call was about.

"That was the hospital," she sighed. "Mom and Dad aren't there anymore. I was about to call you but here you are."

She approached him and gave him a tender kiss. He felt guilty. The age-old expression, "Don't shoot the messenger," was in existence for a reason. The bearer of bad news always felt the anger first, and he dreaded what he needed to tell her.

"They signed out?" He asked as she took a seat on the couch.

"No. That's the thing. They didn't sign out. A nurse was knocked unconscious in their room but other than that there was no sign of a struggle. It's like they walked out."

Easton nodded.

"You don't seem surprised."

"The hospital did call in a report about a disturbance."

"Then why aren't you out looking for them?"

"There are other officers on it. I needed to come and talk to you about something."

"What is it?"

"Well, something disturbing has come up, and I'm hoping you might be able to help me piece it together. Your parents' attack obviously prompted an investigation. That includes all aspects of their lives."

"Okay?" Her eyebrow wrinkled in concentration, and Easton blew out a big breath as he prepared to dive into the rest of the story.

"As a crime scene, records were pulled up on the farmhouse. It's standard procedure. The farm isn't owned by either of your parents."

"It's not?"

"No." He pulled out his computer, typed a few keys and showed her. "Its owner is listed as Dale McDonald since 1985. Have they ever mentioned that name to you before?"

She shook her head. "No, but they are private people. They never discussed their finances with us kids. It wasn't our business. Maybe they're renting."

"That's what I thought at first too," he told her. "Only I can't find any records of a lease agreement."

"Maybe it was under the table in exchange for keeping the place up. That does happen. Why? It's not illegal, is it?"

"No, not by itself," he said. "But when coupled with what came up next, it raised a lot of questions."

"What came up next?"

"Okay. You can't get mad at me."

"What did you do?"

"When we were at the hospital donating blood, I swiped one of your vials when the nurse wasn't looking."

"What?" Her nose wrinkled in disgust. "Why the hell did you steal my blood?"

"I was on alert because of the altercation in your parents' room," he admitted. "The description of everyone about how the attack went down didn't sit right with me. Your dad saying he hit the assailant with a table lamp? They don't have table lamps because they don't have electricity. It would have been an oil lamp, but that should have started a fire. That's weird enough, but it was your mom freaking out when the nurse asked you to donate and kicking you out that cemented it. I wondered if there was something there."

"And?"

"I've come from the lab. Your blood matched something in the system."

"My blood?"

"Mmmhmm."

"What did it match?"

"It's a one hundred percent match to a hair sample from Bethany Patterson."

Her mouth dropped open, but he interjected before she could speak. "How Bethany's DNA got in the database I have no clue, and I don't want to know. I then had it cross-referenced with a blood sample from Susanna Patterson, again don't want to know how we have that, and that showed a maternal match."

"That's not possible," she shook her head. "There must have been a mix-up at the lab."

"I had it checked twice. I also called the hospital and had them compare it with your parents' samples. They were not a match. They showed no relation at all. You're not the same blood type. It's biologically impossible for you to be their daughter."

"No!" she exclaimed and sat back in her seat ramrod straight.

"I then went into the age progression database and ran the photo of Bethany we have on file," he typed on the keyboard and then turned the screen towards her. "According to this, she would look like this now."

The photo was almost a carbon copy of Stacey. The lips were a little fuller than hers, and the hair was red instead of the brown of her childhood, but otherwise it was her.

"I need to know if you knew," he said carefully.

"No!" She jumped to her feet, leaned over him, and slapped him in the face as hard as she could. "I don't know what kind of sick, twisted game you're trying to play here, but it isn't funny!"

She grabbed her keys off the coffee table and stormed out the door.

CHAPTER EIGHTEEN

Stacey sat in her car slumped against the wheel, crying hysterically. Why was Easton being so cruel? There were practical jokes and there was cruelty. This wasn't okay to do to someone.

Suddenly, her body jerked back, and she was surrounded by a swirl of fog and images rushed by her.

She stood behind a car on a dark road with a pretty woman. "Mama, not the potty!" came out of her mouth.

Then she was being shaken awake where she lay in a motel bed with her brother. She would eventually call the man who smiled down at her from under a baseball cap, 'Daddy.'

"Hey there," he'd said. "I bet you like cartoons. There's some on TV next door. Do you want to watch them?"

She'd nodded at him.

"Good. Wake up your brother. Be quiet so we can let your mama sleep a little longer."

That was followed by an image of them sitting in the little back room at the Seaside Motel watching cartoons and snacking on cookies. There was a kind faced, plump woman she would later call her mother there who kept glancing toward the door with a worried expression.

Then she was being snapped at to be still as she wiggled on a stool while chocolate brown dye was massaged into her hair.

There was an image of her and her brother being told their names were Laila and Jason Hunt now. They could never remember so the family name became Petersen. It sounded close enough to Patterson no one questioned it.

Following that was an image of them being pulled from their beds in the middle of the night and driving a long way. Their names were changing again. Now they were Stacey and Gavin Branch. The first time one of them said the wrong name, they'd been smacked in the face.

They were gradually being told it was better to live off the land, and they needed to adapt to life without electricity and running water.

There was a fight about whether to homeschool, and friends being forbidden in the house for the longest time.

There was an intense image of her father shaking her by the shoulders and screaming, "How many times do I have to tell you not to go in the barn?"

Stacey was then catapulted back to her seat in the car. She was in a cold sweat and gasping for air. She could have sworn more than half an hour had passed, but the clock on the dashboard told her it had been less than five minutes.

Nausea rolled in her stomach, and she flung the door open seconds before she vomited.

"Oh my God," she whispered to herself when it was finally over, and she pulled herself back into the car and wiped a hand across her mouth.

Of course. How had she been so stupid? It was right there in front of her the whole time. Other than school photos, she'd never even seen pictures of her or Gavin as kids, certainly not as babies.

"Okay. Okay." She wiped the tears from her eyes and pulled out her phone. Her childhood best friend, Beth Dawson's number was on the display, and her finger hovered above the dial button.

Easton had gotten through to her at the restaurant. She'd looked up Beth's number, but she'd been unable to bring herself to call. Until now.

"Hello?" Her heart soared at the sound of her friend's voice, and she squeezed her eyes tightly closed.

"Beth? It's Stacey. Stacey Branch."

"Stacey? Oh my God, it's so great to hear your voice."

"You too. How are you?"

"Great. I have two kids now."

"Are you still in Virginia?" Stacey couldn't stop the shaking in her voice.

"Stacey, what's wrong?"

"Have you seen the news reports about the car being found in DeSoto?"

"Yeah. That's wild. You wrote an article about it, didn't you?"

"I did. Beth, I—I found out I'm the daughter. The little girl who went missing."

"Are you sure?"

"Blood tests—" she was full on crying now.

"I'm coming. Where are you?"

"I'm about to go back to the farmhouse for answers. Do you remember how to get there?"

"I do, but will you be safe there?"

"It's probably the safest place. It's a crime scene now, so it's roped off."

"Alright. Give me about an hour."

When Beth hung up, Stacey threw the car in reverse and headed toward the farmhouse.

Ten minutes later, when Stacey pulled up to the house, she was startled by how dark and quiet everything was. The farm was normally dark, but this seemed unnatural. She'd expected to see a police presence, but no cruisers were in the area.

She got out of the car and strode toward the kitchen door, which did have crime scene tape across it. She tried the doorknob, and it turned easily in her hands. She ducked down to walk under the tape and pulled out her cell phone to shine it around.

Her mouth went dry as she took in the sight. There was blood all over the floor. Biting down the bile, she turned and made her way to the staircase. There was no point in exploring the first floor. She knew that area like the back of her hand. If there were answers, they would lie in her parents' bedroom.

She made her way to that room and carefully checked the drawers in the end tables and dresser, under the bed, and even behind the bookcase. When all those searches came up clean, she made her way to the closet.

She checked every corner, including the shelf at the top, and found nothing. Feeling defeated, she was about to give up when she stepped on a squeaky board. Aiming her light down, she knelt to the ground and easily pulled the board up.

Jammed under the floorboards was a shoebox that Stacey pulled out and began to sort through. Inside it were tons of papers. There were mostly articles cut from newspapers. There were articles about the car being found from all the surrounding areas newspapers, including her own. There were older articles from Boston newspapers that were extremely yellow and brittle. There were even a couple of articles about the house fire in California.

She was pulled out of her reading by a creak in the hallway. She jerked her up and immediately went to cover the light with her hand, but she wasn't fast enough.

"Stacey?" It was Gavin's voice.

"Damn it, Gavin," she sighed, uncovering the phone. "You scared the shit out of me. What are you doing here?"

He walked into the closet and slid down next to her on the floor. "I parked in the woods. I hoped I could catch them if they came back. I found you instead."

She nodded. It made sense. The hospital would have called him too.

Gavin pointed toward the box that now sat between them. "What have you got?"

"A box of shattered dreams," she said gloomily, continuing to sift through the contents.

He picked up an article from the top and skimmed it. "Shit. You found out."

She snapped her head back toward him in surprise. "You knew? This whole time?"

"Yeah," he said and then immediately shook his head. "No. I mean, not the whole time. But as we got older, I figured out we weren't who they said we were. I didn't know who we were exactly, or how to go about figuring it out, but I knew we were essentially in hiding. Then when that car got pulled out of the lake, and you told me about the owner, I started to wonder. I asked them point blank while I was here with them when you were gone. It was a nasty argument."

"How did you find out?" she asked him in a quiet voice.

"I found some polaroid pictures. There was a woman chained to the wall in a barn. I went out to investigate and peeked through a crack in the door. Dad was in there with her, and he mocked her. She begged him to please let her spend five minutes with her kids. It didn't take a rocket scientist to know that was us."

"How many times do I have to tell you to stay away from the barn?" Her memory of her father's voice screaming at her, now clear in her mind, sent a chill down her spine.

"I stole the keys to the truck and took off."

"That's the real reason he locked you up," Stacey whispered. "To protect his secret."

"Partly," Gavin sighed. "I did go to Mandy's house, and we did drive into the woods. She was my girlfriend at the time. Mom and Dad wouldn't let me date, so it was a big secret. I couldn't process what I'd seen. I know I seemed deranged because I was ranting, and I was trying to force her to let me hold her, but she was scared and kept pulling away. I didn't realize my own strength, and I put bruises on her. I never meant to though. She jumped out of the truck and ran away."

He leaned his head back against the wall and squeezed his eyes shut. "When I got home, I went straight to the barn. I knew I wouldn't get answers from Mom and Dad, so I went to question the woman in there. Only she was gone. Dad came out and found me in there. I confronted him with what I saw. We were arguing loudly about it when we heard a car pulling up. It was Mandy's dad. He was going on about how I tried to rape his daughter, which is not what happened at all. Looking back now, though, I can see why she thought that. Dad had his ace in the hole."

Stacey eyed the box of secrets, unsure of what to ask him next.

"He turned around and smiled at me after Mandy's father left," he said with unblinking eyes. "He told me we were going to the juvenile detention center, and I was going to admit to hurting Mandy and keep my mouth shut about the woman in the barn or he would kill you, and him and Mom would disappear into the night. Everyone would think I'd done it. I couldn't let anything happen to you, Stacey."

A tear rolled down her cheek and she reached over to squeeze his hand. "He actually threatened to kill me?"

He nodded. "I'm sorry. I know it's hard to imagine."

"I shouldn't be surprised. If he's the man I think is, and after everything I've learned in this case, he's deranged. I can't believe I never saw it."

"You didn't have reason to," he told her, squeezing her hand back. "They jumped through hoops to make you happy. Hell, I was happy until that moment. But he turned on me so fast. If he feels he's going to be exposed, he'll turn on you too."

"Well, we're here," Stacey sighed. "We might as well see what else we can learn."

Together, they started going through the box again, more slowly.

"What exactly are we looking for?"

"Anything with names or official. I feel like we're still missing something."

"Ahh, like this?" He pulled out a couple of driver's licenses. Stacey shone her light on them. There were photos of her parents, much younger. The names Marty and Sherry Randall staring out at her didn't surprise her, but the hurt still cut as deep as any knife.

"Shit," she said taking them. "That's what I was afraid of."

"These names are in your investigation?"

"Oh, yeah."

"How did you find out? That we were the missing kids, I mean?"

She snorted derisively. "I donated blood at the hospital. A nurse asked me to. My blood type wasn't a match to Mom or Dad. But it did match Bethany's DNA. Oh, and the age progression photo of her all grown up looks like me."

"Damn. That's a rough way to find out. I'm sorry."

She was about to respond but was cut off by the start of an engine and a squeal of tires from outside.

They both jumped to their feet and raced to the window in time to see the taillights disappearing.

Stacey slammed her fist against the wall. "That was my car."

1996

CHAPTER NINETEEN

Susanna

Susanna felt something cool on her legs. She opened her eyes to blackness. Her throat was raw from screaming so much. She'd blacked out at some point; she wasn't sure when. She wasn't even sure what brought her back around. It was coming back to her now. She was wedged in the trunk of her car, hands and feet tied. Days passed. But what was that feeling? She brought up her legs with much effort and brought them down as hard as she could to a deafening sound of splashing water. Water. The son of a bitch was trying to drown her. She needed to get out of this car.

With minimal movement from her fingers, she fumbled for her makeup bag. If she could get to it, she had a pair of manicure scissors and a nail file. Not the best items for a brave get away, but it was the best she could do. She managed to grasp the strap with one finger and pull it toward her. She fumbled with the zipper with some difficulty. Items spilled from the bag as she fumbled clumsily for something to help her. At long last, she found the tiny manicure scissors and ignoring the searing pain in her wrists from the ropes and fierce cold of the water, turned the scissors upwards and began to saw at the ropes, praying the tiny blades would be enough.

The water level rose slowly as she desperately worked the scissors, cutting the hell out of her hands and wrists, but that wasn't what mattered. She kept an amazing sense of calm for the situation she was in, and she knew it. She had to. There was no other way out of this.

The ropes frayed and there was a slight give to them. She pulled her wrists as hard as she could and managed to free them from the ropes. She ignored the stinging, there wasn't time, and began to release her feet. The water was getting high.

She fumbled for a trunk release switch. Prayed to God there was one. She wasn't having any luck. As her heart beat faster, and her breath caught in her throat, she saw a tiny sliver of light from a hole. Was there a rusty hole? That's where the license plate was. Could she break through? She pushed and had no slack. She felt the cool metal of the license plate. As cool as the water that was now deep in her bones.

She wiggled to the side and kicked as hard as she could twice. The license plate broke off, revealing a hole had started to erode. She could not climb through, but she remembered the trunk didn't lock, and her arm could fit through.

"Please, Jesus," she thought, sticking her arm through the hole, feeling the water rushing her, feeling for the trunk latch. She pushed it and heard the click of release, quickly pulled her arm back inside and pushed against the trunk door as hard as she could. It opened.

She swam out into the deep water, thanking God for the daylight, then made her way toward shore. Her wet clothes clung to her, making her colder as her rubbery legs met earth. She ran as fast as she could on legs suffering from non-use. She found herself back on the road and ran for a building in the distance.

Her heart stopped as she realized she was now behind the motel. That poor receptionist. She hated to think about what she was going to find. But she had to try. She ran to the office door and found it unlocked. She took a deep breath and stepped inside, bracing herself for a massacre. There was no blood. No mess. No sign of a struggle. The lamps were no longer turned on. There were no candles out. The register book was missing from the desk.

"Hello!" she cried out but was met with silence. She ran behind the counter and opened the door beyond it, the door Sherry came from to register her. She found nothing but an empty office, certainly no people.

She ran back out to the reception desk and picked up the telephone receiver. Yes! A dial tone. Without thinking, she dialed the first number she could think of.

"Hello?" came her husband's voice through the receiver. She cried out in joy. A sound never sounded so beautiful to her as in that moment.

"David?" she cried, tears pouring down her face. She felt air flood back into her body and the pressure in her chest lessened.

"Susanna? Oh my God, Baby, it's so good to hear your voice. I've been so worried about you and the kids."

"David, I don't know what to do. Everything is so screwed up."

"What happened? Were you in an accident?"

"No, I was tired and somehow exited the highway and got lost. The car broke down, and some guy came along and helped me. At least I thought he was helping me, but he followed me. David, he kidnapped me and tried to kill me, but I got away. But the kids are gone. I don't know where the kids are!"

"Where are you?"

"I don't know! I don't know!" she said, impatiently. "I got so lost. I'm in a motel somewhere in Virginia. But there's nothing around here. Everything is deserted."

"What's the name of the motel?"

"The Seaside Motel," her voice broke off as she heard a sound approaching. Through the window she saw a red pickup truck with an old toolbox in the bed slowing to a stop. "Oh God."

"What? Susanna? What is it?"

"He's back. He's outside," she whispered.

"You listen to me. I'm going to get you help. You find a place to hide and stay there, alright?'

"Okay."

Susanna hung up the phone and glanced around the room. She heard footsteps approaching. She made a beeline for her only choice, a coat closet in the corner, and prayed no one checked.

Susanna sank to the floor behind some big coats, and peeked through some slats in the door, barely daring to breathe as the office door opened.

"God damn women," the gruff voice muttered, as the man rounded the reception counter, and knelt to the safe below. Susanna could hear the musical beep as he entered a code. "Always wanting something. Should fucking be headed to California by now."

The safe clicked shut. He rose and placed something on the counter. Something Susanna could not see.

"Marty! What's taking so long?" came a woman's voice from outside.

"I'm coming!" he yelled. He stuffed the object in his pocket, then turned to leave the office.

Susanna slowly exited the closet, walking stooped over so not to be seen, then peeked out the window in the front door.

Sherry, the receptionist, stood in front of the truck with her hands on her hips. "Let's get the hell out of here!"

"I've been trying, damn it. I need to check the room one more time," he told her, spitting chewing tobacco on the ground as he passed her.

"You've already checked it twice, Marty!" she called after him as he strode into Room one. "Why do you need to check it again? You did this, Marty, *you* did. We have to get out of here."

He came back out of the room and ran his hands down Sherry's arms. "She doesn't have anyone looking for her. We're okay. I need to go check the bathroom one more time before we go. Will you come with me?"

They both headed into Room one, and Susanna was able to get a better view of the truck. She saw two tiny heads in the cabin. The kids! But she didn't have a car anymore. She couldn't get to them. To hell with that.

She quietly exited the office and slowly walked towards the truck. There was a blue tarp in the bed, and she let out a sigh of relief as she climbed up in the bed under it. Now all there was to do was wait.

Eventually, she heard them head back out towards the truck and get in. Her babies were so close. By God, she wasn't going anywhere this time.

Ashley Bundy

2022

Chapter Twenty

"In breaking news, the towns of DeSoto and Logan's Ridge have been turned upside down. The twenty-six-year-old case of Susanna Patterson, a Boston woman who went missing with her two children has rocked our community."

The screen was filled with images of the Branch farmhouse under blue lights from police vehicles and things being removed from both the house and the barn as the voiceover continued.

"The investigation was reopened officially last week when Patterson's vehicle was recovered from the lake. Throughout the course of the investigation, the children were found, all grown up. One of which is local reporter, Stacey Branch, who is actually Bethany Patterson."

The age progression photos filled the screen. Bethany as a two-year-old, the composite of what she might look like as an adult, and finally a recent photo of Stacey.

"The people whom Stacey believed were her parents are now on the run."

Marty and Sherry Randall's old DMV photos filled the screen, as well as grainy security footage of them sneaking out of the hospital.

"Their real names are Marty and Sherry Randall, but they have also gone under the aliases Martin and Sharon Petersen, and more recently, Paul and Alice Branch. If you see them, please contact the Logan's Ridge Police Department. We will keep you up to date with this rapidly developing case. Susanna Patterson's whereabouts currently remain unknown. We have been unable to reach Stacey or her brother for comment."

Stacey shut off the TV and slammed the remote down on the coffee table. "Vultures," she hissed.

Easton squeezed her shoulder. "Not so easy when the shoe is on the other foot," he joked.

"I still think there's been a mistake," Teresa insisted, and they turned to where she sat in an armchair.

"Mom." Easton said in disbelief. "The bloodwork has been run multiple times on both of them. Stacey and Gavin are Susanna Patterson's children."

"Maybe she abandoned them," Teresa threw up her hands. "All I know is that's not Alice and Paul. I've known them for years and they are two of the best people I know. I could see them taking in abandoned children."

"And not call the police and use assumed names?" Beth Dawson charged back at her from her place on the couch, where she sat with her arm around Stacey's shoulders. "Don't you think it's a little suspicious such a horrible attack happened in the twenty minutes you were gone, neither of them were fatally injured, and the person responsible was nowhere to be found?"

"They were obviously waiting for me to leave."

"I'm sure they were," Gavin snorted as he reentered the room from the bathroom.

Teresa pointed a finger at him. "You might not have a problem talking to your parents with disrespect, but I won't stand for being spoken to like that."

"News flash, lady," Gavin snarled. "They aren't our parents. It's been proven."

"Who fed you, housed you, clothed you, and kept your sorry ass out of trouble?"

"Mom, I think it's time for you to go," Easton said as he made his way to the front door.

Her jaw dropped. "Excuse me?"

"You need to go," he repeated. "I love you, but you are not helping an already tense situation."

She snatched up her purse. "I cannot believe you are taking their side over your own mother's," she hissed as she walked out the door, slamming it behind her.

"Maybe you should take a blood test too, dude," Gavin said slyly. "Make sure she's really your mother. If she's condoning that behavior, she may have done it herself."

Easton shook his head. "I'm sorry about her, guys. It's hard to believe your friend could be capable of something like that."

"It's hard to believe your parents could be too," Stacey whispered.

Stacey and Gavin were now staying with Easton temporarily because both of their apartment buildings had reporters camped outside since the news broke. They rarely left. The media circus has become too unbearable.

"I don't like you told her we were here at all," Gavin said. "No offense. I know she's your mom, but she was also friends with our mom for years. I don't like how easily get it could get back to them where we are."

"I doubt they'll reach out to anyone here," Easton answered.

"Maybe you two should come home with me," Beth said firmly. "I've been gone for years. We lost contact. They wouldn't think of my house."

"No!" Stacey said sharply and squeezed her friend's hand. "You have children. We can't endanger your family."

Beth tightened her lips and nodded.

Stacey shook her head. "You know what I don't get? We were in California. Why'd they come back here? So close to the scene of the crime."

"It's not unusual for perps to return," Easton told her. "Not to mention, after two years, they thought they'd gotten away with it. Everything they knew was out here. They were trying to make everything as familiar to themselves as they could without flat out exposing themselves."

"I don't buy it," Gavin said. "I mean, you guys said that detective was at their house in California right before their 'fire.'" He put up air quotes around his face. "I feel like it had something to do with that. Dad thinks he's smarter than everyone else."

"Marty," Stacey said, leaning back in her seat. "His name is Marty."

"Marty. Sorry. Old habits. He thinks he's smarter than everyone else. It could be that since that detective showed up in California, he decided to come back here thinking it was the last place he'd look for him."

"Except Henry Rusher retired right after that visit."

"Yeah, and what's up with that?" Gavin exclaimed.

"The chief told me today an official request has been put in for FBI assistance. I'm guessing that's one of the things they're going to ask him."

Stacey pulled her knees up to her chest and turned toward her brother. "Can you explain something to me?"

"Of course."

"You seem so content with sitting here and working out the case with us. Which is great. We need to put all the pieces together. I guess I don't understand how you're not fighting to go out searching for Angie."

Gavin clicked his tongue. "Honestly? I'm guessing when we find Mo—when we find Sherry and Marty, we'll find Angie."

"You think he took her?"

"Oh yeah. Dude's hated me for a while because I knew the truth. Well, a half-truth as a kid, but I figured out the whole thing later. She goes missing the day after I ask him if we're those kids? And I was right? There's no way that shit's a coincidence."

"Any luck finding my car?" Stacey asked Easton.

He shook his head. "We traced the tags. Officers pulled over an old lady who nearly pissed her pants. Long story short, they switched the plates."

"So now they're tracing her plates?"

"Yeah, but there haven't been any hits yet."

"Don't you worry about it," Beth said firmly. "You'll be using my car."

"No," Stacey protested. "I couldn't do that."

"Shut up. It's already done. I do need to get back to the hotel, if you're okay."

Stacey smiled. "You trust our motels after everything you've seen?

"Oh, I'm in the next county."

This prompted a belly laugh from everyone in the room.

"Seriously, though. You okay?"

"I'm okay."

"Alright. Then I'm gonna go get a few hours of sleep." She dug her keys out of her purse and tossed them to Stacey.

"Do you need an escort?" Easton asked her.

"Nah. I'll take a rideshare. You guys need your rest too."

CHAPTER TWENTY-ONE

David

David Patterson walked out of the air terminal, glanced down at the note he'd scribbled information on, and scanned the line of cars.

He'd been shaking ever since he received the phone call. His kids were alive. After all this time. His kids had been found.

Tia didn't want him to go. She'd screamed at him as he'd packed a small bag saying they were adults now, and he didn't need to rush to them, but she didn't understand. When your children disappear in a puff of smoke, you give up hope, and when they're finally found, it doesn't matter how much time has passed. They are still your children. You still need to hold them in your arms.

He spotted the blue Taurus a few car lengths back, verified the license plate, and trotted over to it. He opened the back door and tossed his bag in before climbing into the front seat.

"Thank you for being so patient," he said. "There was a hold-up in the terminal."

"No problem." The driver glanced at him and the breath momentarily left his body.

"Susanna?"

She didn't smile, but she didn't grimace either. She was in rough shape. She'd lost a lot of weight and now was much too skinny. Her cheeks were sunken in, and there was a large scar along the side of her face. Dark circles shadowed her eyes, and her hair hung limply in her eyes.

"Hey, David," she said simply and drove.

His heart thundered crazily in his chest as a million emotions flooded through him. First, relief she was okay too, and then suspicion that maybe the whole thing was a trick to get him here and hurt him.

"So, umm, the police didn't call me?"

"The police called you. Which worked out well for me," she told him. "I was prepared to say I was an officer when I called, but you were already in such a panicked state saying you were booking a ticket. All I had to do was say I'd pick you up from the airport. Here I am."

"I'm so confused." His mouth was dry, and he tried to remember how to breathe correctly. "So, that detective was right all those years ago? When he said you faked the whole thing and ran off with them?"

She snorted. "What exactly did the police say when they called?"

"Not much. Just that the kids were found, and they're alive. Something about a blood test."

She shook her head. "Did you not turn on the TV? It's all over the news down here."

"Of course I didn't. I immediately packed and went straight for the airport."

Susanna sighed. "Well, whatever this detective told you back then was all wrong. We were all kidnapped by a sadistic couple."

"The police didn't say anything about finding you though."

"They didn't," she let out a long breath. "They locked me up and raised the kids as their own. Mason and Bethany eventually forgot about me."

"But they let you go?"

"No." She shook her head. "A few days ago, a girl I'd never seen showed up. She had the key to the cuffs and let me go. She told me to run away."

"Was it Bethany?"

"No. She was older than Bethany. But she still seemed to know everything. I did what she said. I ran into the woods. I assumed she was behind me, but she wasn't. When I noticed she wasn't there, I climbed a tree to take in my surroundings. I must have fallen asleep. When I woke up it was dark, and I was still in the tree. I saw a car outside the farmhouse I was at. I took it."

"This car is stolen?"

"I needed to get out of there."

David's arm shot forward, and he opened the glove box to riffle through things inside.

"What are you looking for?"

"Identification. We have to return the car. I'll rent one, but we can't keep a hot car. It makes you guilty. Besides, it probably belongs to the girl who helped you."

He found the registration. "Susanna, do you know whose car this is?"

"No. I snatched it and ran."

"This is Stacey Branch's car. She's a reporter who has been covering your case. She flew out to see me AND Mallory. Why the hell was she at the place you were being held captive?"

Susanna's eyes darted over to him. "I didn't know you'd seen her. According to the news, though, Stacey Branch *is* Bethany."

"What?" This was getting weirder by the second. "Wait, hang on. How are you seeing the news?"

"It's been on the radio a lot. Plus, I've walked through town, listening to conversations."

"No one's noticed?"

"Being a dead woman has its advantages."

She pulled the car over on the side of the road and took in a deep, shuddering breath.

"This is where it all started."

David took in their surroundings. It was an empty expanse of land, nothing on either side. "This is where...?"

She nodded. "The car broke down. Imagine it pitch black. No clue where I was. I thought I was saved when the man showed up. Even though he did creep me out. Why didn't I listen to my gut?"

David was about to say something reassuring when there was a blip, and blue and red lights shone in the rearview mirror.

"Great," David whispered to himself.

An officer approached the car and knocked on the driver's side window.

Susanna took a deep breath and rolled down the window.

The officer bent at the waist to see in the car. He had a smirk on his face that instantly fell when he saw them. It was as if he expected them to be someone else.

"There's an APB out on this car, folks. I'm going to have to ask you to step out of the vehicle. Slowly. Where I can see your hands."

They both did as the officer asked, and David was directed around the front of the car to stand next to Susanna.

"Identification?"

David slowly pulled out his wallet and passed it to the officer.

He flicked his eyes up at David. "David Patterson, huh? Well, we kind of figured you'd be out this way soon. Thought you'd be alone though."

He passed the wallet back to David and turned his gaze back to Susanna. "Ma'am. Your identification?"

Susanna shook her head and let a tear roll down her cheek.

"You don't have it? And you were driving this vehicle?"

She nodded and blew out a breath, hanging her head.

"Officer, please. I can explain this," David said, but the officer held up a hand to silence him without taking his eyes off Susanna.

He studied her face closer, and then took in the rest of her bedraggled appearance, his eyes falling on the raw markings around her wrists.

"My God," he whispered. "You're that missing woman. Susanna Patterson. Aren't you?"

She took another deep breath and nodded.

Susanna

Susanna sat on a couch in an office with her legs pulled up against her chest.

David was taken to a separate room while the female officer spoke with her and gave her fresh clothes. They were only sweats, but they felt nice on her skin. She couldn't remember the last time she'd been given something new to wear. The woman was extremely nice, but she hadn't asked any of the questions Susanna expected. She'd wanted to photograph the marks on Susanna's body but hadn't asked for any details.

There was a quick knock on the door and an officer walked in with David trailing behind him holding a fast-food bag and a large soda.

"Susanna. I'm Officer Easton Gates. You can call me Easton. I won't tell anyone."

She nodded and gave a half-hearted smile.

A woman then walked into the room with a no-nonsense expression on her face, hair slicked back into a tight bun and wearing a sharp blue pantsuit.

"This is Detective Carmen Reynolds," Easton introduced her. "She arrived from the FBI."

"Hello, Susanna," she said.

Susanna nodded and stared at her feet. She felt intimidated being here, like she'd done something wrong.

"I'm going to need to talk to you about what happened to you. If you're more comfortable, we can have your ex-husband wait outside."

She wasn't surprised to hear her call David her ex-husband. Years had passed after all. It still felt strange though. When she'd gone missing, they were still married.

"I brought you some food," David said, giving her a smile and holding up the bag.

She rose from her seat on the couch and made her way to sit opposite the officers at the desk instead and took the bag from David.

"It is okay if she eats, right?" David asked, turning toward Detective Reynolds.

"Of course," she said, setting up a tape recorder and getting her notepad out.

"Susanna?" Officer Gates gently prodded. "Would you prefer he be here for this part or not?"

"He can stay," she sighed. "It concerns him too."

David sank down in the seat next to her and smiled again. "Thank you."

"So, I see the patrol officer picked you up on Route 6. You were parked on the side of the road. He ran the plates and saw it was a stolen vehicle."

"I'm not a thief," she said defensively. "It's just I was in the middle of nowhere and that was my only chance to get away."

Easton smiled at her. He had kind eyes. "Given the circumstances, you are not in any trouble for taking the car. We want to know what happened."

She nodded she understood and opened the bag of fast food from David. The smell of a cheeseburger hit her in the face, and it smelled like heaven.

"Why were you on Route 6?"

"That's where it all started," she said and took a small bite of the burger.

"We think we know part of the story," he told her. "Because you called your husband from the Seaside Motel but there were a lot of missing pieces. Understandable of course. Emotions would have been high. You said something on the phone about your car breaking down. Was that on route six?"

Susanna nodded. "I had a bad feeling, but I didn't know what to do. This man showed up, and I thought it was a blessing at first because he offered to check the engine. Then he started acting weird."

"In what way?" Detective Reynolds asked.

"Talking about how women shouldn't be driving around in the dead of night in broken-down cars, and my husband should have a handle on me. As bad as that was, it was nothing compared to his face when Bethany got out of the car and told me she needed to pee. He was livid."

"Okay. What happened next?"

"After Bethany finished doing her business the guy tells me the car is basically shot. I wouldn't make it back to the highway, but I could make it into town and trade it in at a local dealer. He said there was a motel right down the road from there. He gave me directions and then he let me go. I actually thought I misjudged him."

The room was quiet as she took another bite, and they waited for her to continue.

"I went to this motel, checked in, put the kids to bed, showered and went to bed myself. I was awoken not long after by a noise. The kids were gone and the man from the road was in my room. I was already tied up."

She felt David stiffen next to her, and he pulled in a deep breath.

"He ranted about how I was a horrible mother, and he was doing them a favor. Then he put me in the trunk of my car. I don't know how long I was there. Days it felt like. Then he put it in the water. I fought my way loose and managed to get out of the car. I ran up to the motel, but no one was there, so I called David."

"Why didn't you call the police?"

She shrugged her shoulders. "Adrenaline, I guess. It happened, and I was worried about my kids."

"Okay," Easton said. "So, we're up to your phone call to David. After that, your trail ran cold. Can you tell us what happened?"

"I heard a car approaching, so I hid in the coat closet. I could hear them arguing. He came back inside and fiddled around with the safe. I guess they came back for it."

"Did you see what it was?"

She shook her head. "When he went back outside, I came out of my hiding spot. I saw through the window the woman talking to him was the receptionist that checked me in. I thought he'd killed her. Then they went into a room, and I ran outside. I could see the kids' heads through the window, but I didn't have time to pull them out, so I got in the back of the pickup. Under a tarp."

"I guess he found you," David said.

"Oh yeah. He found me."

Susanna's muscles screamed from being bounced around for so long. She'd hit her head a few times, giving her a massive headache. She tried to straighten her leg out and bit back a scream from the pain in her knee.

The truck finally pulled to a stop. She had no clue how long she'd been in the bed of the truck. She placed a hand over her mouth to silence any gasping breaths she may have as the doors to the truck were opening.

"Do you need to go to the bathroom?" Sherry asked.

Both kids exclaimed they did, and Bethany chimed in to say she was hungry.

"We're not stopping to eat," the man, Marty, growled out. "You'll have to wait."

"Marty," Sherry's voice was calm. "They're little. They need to eat more. I'll grab them some snacks while we're inside."

"Junk food?" he said. Susanna could hear the sneer in his voice. "That's how you want to start our lives as parents?"

"It won't be an everyday thing, Marty. But it'll keep them satisfied until our next stop."

"Fine. Don't make a habit of it."

There were shuffling footsteps moving away and scraping at the side of the truck.

Gas station. They were at a gas station! Susanna's heart leapt in her chest. That meant someone was nearby. She could get help. She'd have to play her cards right, though. Where was he?

She tried to maneuver her head gradually to peek around the edge of the tarp, but she couldn't see anything except the night sky above.

Then the truck shook as something landed in the back and she felt something on each side of her body.

"How the fuck did you get out of the trunk?" he snarled at her, ripping the top of the tarp back.

He wasn't wearing his baseball cap anymore, and with the moon as a backdrop he seemed absolutely deranged.

He moved to put his hands around her throat when a voice called out.

"Everything okay, Mister?"

He checked over his shoulder and waved a hand. "Yeah! Almost lost the load! Have to tie it down!"

He grabbed rope from nearby.

153

Susanna made to scream to the stranger, but Marty gently popped her cheek.

"If you say one word, I'll kill them both. You know that, right?"

She believed him. This man had already committed the kind of atrocities she thought only existed in books and bad horror movies. He was capable of anything.

He didn't pull the tarp back any further, she figured to avoid her being seen but tied the tarp tight to the sides of the truck.

"You know, I gotta give you credit," he said under his breath. "You're smarter than I thought you were. Getting out of the trunk like that and onto my truck. Under other circumstances, I might respect you. 'Course you're still dumb as a box of rocks. That's why you don't deserve those babies. You'll see. I'm gonna make you see."

There was a sound as footsteps approached. "Marty, what're you doing back there?" Sherry asked.

"We have a stowaway."

"What?" Then a face peered over the side of the truck and Sherry's eyes widened. "What?" Her voice was shrill.

"Shut up," Marty hissed. "Do you want to be noticed? There's already someone nosing around. Put the kids in the truck. We gotta get outta here."

Without saying another word to her, Marty threw the tarp back over her face.

David's head drooped in his hands. "You were a few feet away from someone, and you didn't call out for help?"

"He said he'd kill the kids!" Her eyes were hurt.

"It was a bluff," he told her gently. "The kids were inside the gas station. You said so yourself. He'd have to go hunt them down, which would leave you unattended and draw attention to himself."

"So, this is my fault?" she snapped.

"I'm not saying that."

"It sure as hell sounds like it."

"That's enough," Detective Reynolds said sharply. "It's not doing any good to place blame and point fingers. We need to go through what happened so we can try to find them and stop them from doing this to anyone else."

Easton's phone rang, and he apologized to them as he answered.

"Gates."

He listened to the other person talking and interjected. "Okay, okay, Stace. Calm down. I'll be right there."

David sat forward in his chair, and Susanna's hand flew to her throat.

Easton hung up and rose to his feet, grabbing a coat from a rack behind his desk. "Sorry, folks. I need to go check on something quickly. I'll be back shortly."

"Stacey?" David rose to his feet as well. "Was that Bethany?"

Easton cast his eyes down.

"Was it Bethany?" David was more insistent now.

"Yes," Easton said softly. "She's not in danger but something happened I need to document. I'll be right back."

"I'm coming with you."

"Me too," Susanna said, rising to her feet.

"Like hell," Easton growled. "This is a police matter. You two stay here and finish your interview."

"Look here, sonny," David wagged a finger at him. "I'm coming. I haven't seen my children in twenty-six years, and I'll be damned if anyone keeps me away. If that's where you're going, that's where I'm going."

"Well, you did see Bethany a week ago," Susanna said sheepishly.

"Yeah, well. I didn't know it was her, so it doesn't count."

Easton turned to Detective Reynolds, but her response was not what anyone expected.

"It's okay," she said. "I need a debriefing from your chief anyway. We can finish up later."

Easton sighed. "You keep a low profile and do what I say. Got it?"

"Got it."

They both followed him out of the building and to his cruiser where they all piled inside.

"Why are you calling her Stacey?" Susanna asked, clipping her seatbelt. "Her name is Bethany."

"She doesn't remember being anyone other than Stacey," Easton said as he pulled away from the police station. "I know she's Bethany to you, but it's still going to take them time to adjust to another life.'

"He's right." David glanced at her in the mirror. "If we want to be a part of their lives now, we have to go at their pace."

Susanna crossed her arms over her chest. She didn't like this.

Chapter Twenty-Three

"Stacey? Gavin?" Easton called when he walked into his apartment with Susanna and David trailing behind him.

Gavin walked out of the kitchen, drying his hands on a towel. "Stacey's in the shower."

Easton saw Susanna's face light up as she saw him, but he jumped into cop mode to avoid her throwing herself at him. Baby steps.

"Stacey said something was slid under the door?"

"Oh, yeah." Gavin walked over to the coffee table and picked up a plastic bag with a piece of paper in it. "Stacey touched it when she saw it on the floor, but once she realized what it was, she said we should bag it."

Easton took the bag from him and saw it was a note. *"You ungrateful shits can forget about the baby."*

"How far along is she?"

"I don't know. She thought about six weeks. Not sure if that's right."

"Can you get me the number for her OB/GYN?"

"Yeah." Gavin pulled out his cell phone and sank down into a chair.

"Did you hear that?" Susanna said in a half whisper, nudging David's arm. "We have a grandbaby."

Gavin turned to her. "Excuse me?"

"It's us, baby," Susanna rushed forward and sat down on the sofa opposite him and reached for his hand. "It's Mom and Dad."

Gavin stared at Easton who nodded his head. He turned back to Susanna and pulled his hand back from her. "I'm sorry for what happened to you. I really am. Those people are twisted as hell. I know that. But I don't know you. Hell, I haven't seen you since I was what, four years old?"

"Three."

"Exactly." He nodded at her. "I'm not your little boy."

He then turned back to his phone, and Susanna's face fell.

Easton's heart fell into the pit of his stomach at the hurt on the woman's face. This was exactly why he hadn't wanted to bring Susanna and David with him.

The sound of a door opening in the back of the apartment reached them, and Stacey walked out wearing a bathrobe and rubbing a towel over her hair.

She stopped dead in her tracks when she saw David and Susanna standing in the living room. A spark of recognition passed between her and David, and they nodded at each other.

Susanna rose from the couch and turned toward Stacey, but she didn't approach her. The sting of Gavin's rejection was still fresh on her face.

"Stacey, you've already met David. This is Susanna," Easton awkwardly offered in way of introductions.

"What?" she said under her breath. There was no malice in her tone, and he could understand why she hadn't immediately recognized the woman. Susanna was barely recognizable. "When?"

"Patrol picked her up today. In your car."

"You're the one who took my car?"

"I didn't know it was yours," Susanna said shyly. "I never would have left."

"Alright, Easton," Gavin interrupted, and Easton's cell phone chirped. "I sent you the doctor's contact info."

"I'm gonna send this into the office and have them reach out. See if we can get the record to update her report. I think the five of us should have a little powwow."

He hit a few buttons on his phone before putting it away and then turned to the group. "This is the first time you've all been in a room in nearly three decades. Does anyone have anything to say?"

Gavin stared at his lap, clearly in no mood to engage.

"Do—Do either of you remember anything?" Susanna asked sheepishly.

Stacey sighed and moved to the couch and sank down on it. "Little pieces now. I didn't realize it before but now there are things that make sense knowing."

"Like what?" David asked and took a seat in another cushy armchair.

"Well, off the top of my head, the first time we watched a movie in school was in the third grade. The teacher wheeled in this big box TV. I should have been fascinated by it. Sherry and Marty didn't have a television in the house, and we didn't have that kind of childhood. Yet, I had distinct memories of cartoons and fairy tale princesses. I was forced to start dying my hair at a crazy young age. I'm not even sure when it started. I don't remember not doing it."

"But do you remember anything about—us?" Susanna asked.

Stacey shook her head. "Just one comment. No context. I remember saying, 'not the potty.'"

A tear rolled down Susanna's cheek. "I hate that's the only memory you have of us. That was that night. We were broken down on the side of the road and that awful man was working under the hood. I took you behind the car to go."

"What about you?" David asked Gavin.

Gavin almost didn't answer and then finally blew out a breath. "I figured it out before Stacey. Not our identities. I didn't know that. But I knew we weren't who they said we were. I knew there was a secret. I saw you once," he gestured toward Susanna, "in the barn."

She put a hand to her mouth. "You saw that?"

He nodded. "I spied on my dad. We weren't supposed to be out there. I ended up getting into trouble, and he found a way to send me away for a while. I tried telling a couple of people there what I saw but no one listened. When I came back, I went straight to the barn, but you weren't there." He shrugged his shoulders. "I was a kid. I didn't know what else I could do."

"It's not your fault. I was still there. You couldn't see me. He built a secret room under the barn. A little at a time. Kept his work bench over the entrance."

Easton nodded. "We found it. There was a plethora of evidence."

"Any sign of Angie?" Gavin asked.

Easton shook his head. "It doesn't look like she was ever kept there."

Gavin ran his hands through his hair. "I really thought he had her. Maybe she did just leave."

"No." David's voice was strong and assertive. "That's what everyone tried to convince me about Susanna, but I knew in my gut she didn't leave on her own. If you feel the same thing about your wife, don't stop fighting."

Gavin gave him a quick nod but didn't respond.

Susanna studied the walls. "Do you have any pictures? Of you two on your wedding day? I'd love to see them."

"This is actually my apartment," Easton chimed in. "We brought them here temporarily because of the press."

"I do have a picture though." Gavin surprised them all by opening his wallet to pull out a photo. "It's not of the wedding but—" he passed it to Susanna, who took it happily. She put a hand to her mouth, and David shot up from his seat to peer over her shoulder.

"This is her," Susanna whispered. Then she said it again with a stronger voice. "This is the woman who saved me!"

Easton snatched the photo from her grasp to stare at it, but Susanna stared at Gavin. "That girl is your wife?"

"She released you?" He was as shocked as her.

"And she's missing?" her voice cracked.

Easton continued to flick his eyes from the players before him to Gavin and Angie smiling on a miniature golf course. He was going to get whiplash from this case.

Chapter Twenty-Four

Carmen Reynolds

Detective Carmen Reynolds slammed her phone down and rolled her shoulders to crack her neck. This case had been butchered so many times, it was a fucking train wreck. It was honestly a miracle the three missing people survived. The justice system failed them at every turn.

She'd double and triple checked and been astonished to learn law enforcement never submitted a request for FBI assistance. A missing person's case involving minor children that crossed state lines should have been handed off. Hell, even the local police department took way too long to call them in, but at least they finally did the responsible thing.

In the short amount of time she'd been on the case, she'd uncovered a ton of information. It was there if anyone bothered to properly look.

Her email chirped in the browser, and she moved to open it, but was interrupted by the chief sticking his head in the door.

"Detective Reynolds?"

"Yes?"

"Suspect is here."

She grinned. "Showtime." She locked down her computer before following him to an interrogation room.

The man sitting at the end of the table rose when she and the chief entered. He was older than she expected and wore a tailored suit with elbow patches.

"Former Detective Rusher?" She took his offered hand. "I'm Detective Carmen Reynolds. We appreciate you coming so fast."

"Of course. Being the lead investigator on this case when it was first reported makes me the natural choice to assist."

"Do you mind if I record this?" she asked, gesturing toward her tape recorder as she took her seat.

"Not at all." He straightened his tie.

Arrogant little shit, she thought to herself. She would enjoy tearing him apart.

"You were a high-ranking detective with the Boston P.D. for many years. A perfect record, I see. That's impressive."

He shrugged his shoulders. "Some of them took a while. But I was always like a dog with a bone during my investigations."

"It must sting to have this one reopened then?"

"Well, I am surprised," he said. "It seemed open and shut at the time. But clearly, I missed something, and that's on me. I'll do anything I can to help."

"It seems odd to me you never requested assistance from the FBI."

"Well, I didn't see the need at the time. There were issues within the marriage. An affair. The sister said she planned on leaving him. Kind of an elaborate way to do it, but people leave marriages every day."

"Did you investigate Marty and Sherry Randall? Interview them?"

"No. They'd left town before we got out there."

"You didn't find that strange?"

He smiled. "People are allowed to move, Detective Reynolds."

"You didn't investigate them at all?"

"Well, I spoke to their employers. Susanna was in the register. We knew she'd checked in and checked out. There was no reason to believe they were covering anything up. We were told there was a death in the family, and they'd relocated due to that."

"Did you verify that?"

"No. As I said, they weren't suspects. I wasn't going to chase a grieving family across the country for no reason."

"Really?" She furrowed her eyebrows and checked her file. "There was an expense report put in for a trip to California a week before your retirement."

"Yes. I had to go to California for another case." He leaned forward. "You know, I don't want to tell you how to do your job, but I thought I should let you know. You might want to talk to Stacey Branch. Writing articles about the case when she's one of the concerned parties all along? Seems impossible she didn't have any idea what was going on."

"I'll take that under advisement."

"Also, I saw her in California a couple of weeks ago. She was with one of your officers." He smirked at the chief. "Did the rule on engaging with press on active cases change?"

"Oh," Detective Reynolds fluttered her eyelashes. "What were you doing in California?"

"I was visiting a college buddy of mine."

Bingo. You put your balls right in the vice grip, you shit, she thought to herself. "Your college buddy was in the hotel room across from Stacey Branch? That's an awful big coincidence."

He sputtered. "Well, no. I stayed at that hotel. I was surprised to hear her name, I'll tell you. That's no crime."

"No," she agreed. "But you checked in right after her, got the room across from her, and checked out after her. Plus, phone records indicate that a few days prior, you were relentlessly trying to reach her at the newspaper office."

Rusher's eyes went wide, and his lips turned up in a snarl. "Are you investigating *me*?"

"The ball got dropped on this case twenty-six years ago. It's our job to investigate everyone. You understand."

"So, 1998. The Patterson case is closed right after you return. Even though you were there investigating someone else."

"Yes." He said through gritted teeth. "But the timing was merely a coincidence. I had to close out my files." She could see his knuckles were turning white.

"It's interesting Jerry Riley said you came out to see him during that trip. He's Sherry's brother-in-law. But, of course, you know that. Says he pointed you to where they were staying."

"That's a damn lie," he hissed. "Am I under arrest?"

"Oh, yes," she said pleasantly. "We have you for twelve counts of misconduct so far. Charges are growing by the hour."

"I want a lawyer."

"Of course. Chief? Read him his Miranda rights and see he receives council."

She rose from her seat and walked out the door.

"That was incredible," one of the officers that been in the room observing told her as they walked back to the desk she was used. "You wiped the smile right off his face."

"Yes, thank you," she logged back into her computer and went to check her email. What she saw made her blood run cold. "Get me the chief. Now."

"Right away, ma'am," the officer said before he scurried off.

Detective Reynolds reread the email three times. Shit. The job just got more complicated.

"You wanted to see me, Detective Reynolds?" the chief approached her.

"Where did you say the Branch's are staying?"

"With Officer Gates. Why?"

"Look at this," she leaned back so he could read her email. He went white. "This is certain?"

"DNA hit. What do you know about the missing girls?"

"Not much, none of them were from our county. There were six young women between the ages of eighteen and twenty-five who went missing last year. All lived in apartments. All were snatched from their homes. No bodies were ever found."

"According to this, the perp only left DNA at one of the crime scenes, but nothing flagged in the database until now. Do you have any current missing person's cases? Even if they don't fit the M.O."

"One. Gavin Branch's wife."

"Get me her file."

Without another word, the chief turned on his heel.

Chapter Twenty-Five

Stacey tossed and turned that night. Her mind swirled in a million different directions. She punched her pillow to fluff it up and rearrange its position under her head.

Easton's apartment was small, and now extremely over cramped with the five of them staying in it. Stacey and Susanna were given the single bedroom to share, but Stacey was not ready to share a bed. She felt bad for Susanna spending so much time chained up and gave her the bed, making herself a pallet on the floor.

She couldn't sleep as everything kept going through her mind. Every moment over the past two weeks kept replaying in her mind like a movie, and something gnawed at her brain. She squeezed her eyes shut and concentrated with all her might to will the pieces to make sense, but they remained a jumble.

Finally, Stacey grunted in frustration and threw her blanket off her to get up. She tip-toed out of the room to not wake up the guys, who were bunking in the living room. She went into the kitchen and grabbed an iced coffee from the refrigerator. If she wasn't going to be able to sleep, she might as well be able to concentrate.

She took a seat at the kitchen table and pulled a file over to flip through it. It was a file for their case. She was a little surprised Easton brought it home and left it out in the open, but a lot had been happening.

Little by little, she studied the pages. She read notes from Henry Rusher. There was little there from the earlier part of the case. Most of the file was everything that had been uncovered since the car was pulled from the lake. She gulped when she saw the lab reports from the items she'd submitted. So, they knew about that. She guessed she should be grateful no one had confronted her about it yet.

Even as she flipped through the pages, Stacey still felt she was missing something obvious. When she got to the final page, several things stood out that made every nerve ending she had freeze.

There were photos of the fortress where Susanna was held captive. The photos started at the entrance to the barn, leading into one with the work bench moved away from the wall. There was a hole in the floor, leading down some steps. The next photos were of a room she'd never seen before with chains nailed into the wall, a key discarded on the dirt floor, and various bits of debris. A bucket stood in the corner, which she imagined held human waste.

Bright red exclamation points were flashing in her head like neon lights. There was something about this her brain was trying to alert her to, but she didn't understand. She glanced down to a handwritten note under the photos.

Pregnancy test negative. The note was scrawled quickly, circled in red ink with a question mark next to it. Then the flashes hit her.

"I saw him in the barn," Gavin said.

"Her phone was sitting on your workbench," Easton's voice echoed.

"A girl showed up with the key," Susanna's voice overlayed.

"Oh my God," Stacey said when the lightbulb hit her. She grabbed her keys and made her way for the door.

Chapter Twenty-Six

Stacey wasn't sure what to do when she pulled into the auto shop. It was the middle of the night, and she hadn't thought of going through Gavin's things to find a key, but she was surprised to see the door was unlocked when she pulled on it.

She flipped on the light switch and made her way for Gavin's workbench to run her hands over the surface. She didn't know what she was looking for but there had to be something. There was no way to measure how much time she'd spent in here, standing in this very spot with her brother. Had anything ever stood out?

Stacey scanned the walls and corners, searching for security cameras, but they weren't there. That would have made her life so much easier, but she knew by now something like that was a pipe dream.

She got down on the floor and searched for any cracks or creases that may indicate a secret opening, but there was none.

She was about to get back to her feet when the light shone off something behind the bench, partially blocked by a box. She scooted the box over and gasped when she saw a hinge.

Stacey shot to her feet and immediately put her fingers to the back of the bench to pull it forward, but immediately realized it was part of the wall. She squeezed her eyes shut and took slow, deliberate breaths. In her mind's eye, she recalled him running his hand down the link of a hammer when she'd entered the room.

She ran her hands over surfaces again, going slower this time until she felt something unusual with a hammer hanging off the pegboard. She pulled it and there was a mechanical squeal as the bench moved away from the wall.

"Son of a bitch," she whispered to herself and stepped behind it. There were fluorescent lights in the ceiling that were already lit. She slowly made her way along the wall until she came to a larger room with a similar setup to the photos from the file. There were several sets of chains in the wall, and in the corner, there was a woman sitting on the floor. Her knees were drawn up to her chest, and her head rested against her knees. A chain was wrapped around one wrist.

"Angie?" Stacey said in surprise.

The woman raised her head and squinted her eyes against the light. "Stacey?"

Stacey raced forward and examined her sister-in-law's wrist. The cuffs were tight, and the skin was starting to rub raw.

"How'd you find me?" Angie asked.

"A lot's happened while you've been in here," Stacey said. "Are you okay? Do you know where the key is?"

"Gavin has it."

Stacey's heart dropped. "It was Gavin that put you in here?"

Angie nodded.

"Are you okay? Did he hurt you?"

"I'm fine. Just a little thirsty. There're water bottles in the fridge over there, but I can't reach it. He usually checks on me, but it's been a while."

Stacey turned in the direction Angie nodded and saw a mini fridge in the opposite corner. She went over and grabbed a water bottle, opened it, and handed it to Angie who took it with her free hand.

"Okay," Stacey sat on the ground and raked her eyes over every surface, trying to think of her next move. She pulled out her cell phone but didn't have any bars.

"Is Gavin okay?" Angie asked.

"He did this to you and you're still checking on him?"

"It's not what you think, Stacey," Angie shook her head. "He's not a monster. Do I seem hurt?"

Stacey couldn't deny she looked okay, but she couldn't wrap her head around what she was seeing.

"What is going on?"

Angie leaned her head against the wall. "It started with the best of intentions. It really did. Gavin told me early in our relationship about the woman in the barn. He was broken and didn't know what to do. We formed a plan."

"When he came home from the detention center, Gavin told me the woman was gone."

"That's true," Angie nodded. "Very true. But Paul slipped up. He was—well, he was Paul, and he insinuated that woman was still his prisoner. He practically rubbed it in Gavin's face. We knew she couldn't be far. He was too cocky for that. It was a matter of finding her. We started surveillance, and it didn't take long to notice all the suspicious trips he still took to the barn. She was still in there. Hidden.

"We leased this building, put in the secret door, set it up as close to his torture chamber as we could. It was supposed to be an irony thing. The eventual plan was to capture them, lock them in here, rescue the woman, and go to the cops."

"So, what happened?"

"A lot of things," Angie chuckled. "Alice's stroke. You moving in. We couldn't snoop as much. At the very least, we had to be more careful. Then the car was found."

Stacey watched Angie's face change. Sadness washed over her features and sorrow swam in her eyes.

"Gavin broke. Once your article dropped, he panicked. He wanted to abort the plan."

"Why?"

"I think he thought you would be blamed. I'm not sure. He stopped making sense. But when he pieced together who you all were, he didn't think he could stand to see her. I said I'd do it, but he kept saying no. I couldn't leave that poor girl in captivity. Not once I found where Paul hid the key. And not upon figuring out she was Gavin's real mother. So, I went rogue."

She sighed. "I watched from the woods and waited for Gavin to leave their house that night, waited for them to go to bed, retrieved the key, and let her out. It was so easy. I didn't go home that night. I drove around and tried to figure out my next move. I came to the shop the next morning and told him what I'd done. He was so angry. He wrestled me to the ground and dragged me in here. He said it was to keep me safe."

"But he hasn't hurt you?"

Angie shook her head. "Not once. I think he mentally broke from everything. He was being pulled in a million different directions and snapped. I don't agree with him, but I do understand it. He was coming in every few hours, bringing me food, giving me water, letting me use the bathroom."

She gestured to a doorway that initially Stacey completely missed. It was complete with a toilet and shower. "But he hasn't been here for a while. I've actually been getting worried."

"A lot happened on the outside," Stacey told her. "Everyone learned the truth; our parents went on the run after a brutal attack. That wasn't you?"

Angie shook her head. "No, I've been in here."

"Well, anyway, to make a long story short, we've been under police protection since our real identities have been discovered."

"But you're here."

"I snuck out. He's been kind of cagey and things clicked inside. I had a gut feeling I needed to come here."

There was a loud scraping, and she recognized the sound as the door. Stacey ran toward it as it slammed closed, and she banged her hands against the door. "Gavin! Gavin! Open the door!"

"I can't let you out, Stacey." The voice did not belong to Gavin. It was the soft, gentle voice of the woman she'd always believed to be her mother.

"What the hell are you doing here?"

"Your father and I are laying low in the office."

"That bastard is not my father!" Stacey screamed and banged her hand against the door.

"Okay. Okay. You're right. Anyway, you're lucky. We didn't know about this door. He's gone to get us food. If he knows you're there, it won't be good. He wants you dead, Stacey. Just don't make noise. I'll find a way to pull the switch before we leave. Until then, be quiet. And, I know it doesn't change anything, but I do love you."

Stacey banged her hand against the door again.

"Be quiet," Alice said again. "I can hear him outside."

"Shit," Stacey hissed and sank down on the floor next to Angie.

"Just try to relax," Angie told her. "There's nothing to do until Gavin comes. We have to wait it out."

Stacey shook her head. "No. No, there has to be something that can be done." She got up and searched their room.

Easton

Easton jerked awake in his recliner. Susanna stood over him with her hand on his shoulder.

"What? What is it?" he asked her.

"Stacey and Gavin are gone," she told him.

"What? What do you mean gone?"

"I woke up to go to the bathroom, and Stacey wasn't there. I came out here to find her and Gavin's gone too."

Easton strode toward the couch where Gavin had been sleeping and saw she was right. The blankets were thrown back.

He rose to his feet and walked through the apartment, checking the kitchen and bathroom. In the kitchen, he saw his case file opened on the table next to a half empty bottle of iced coffee.

Shit. He'd forgotten to put it in the safe. He went over to see what they'd been looking at and saw the file was open to the pictures from the secret room in the barn.

What exactly about this picture would cause them to leave without waking anyone up?

Easton grabbed his cell phone to put in a call to the station as David followed Susanna into the kitchen. "Hey, it's Easton Gates. Is the chief in? What? Slow down. I can't understand you."

He paused and listened to the other person talking fast and breathing heavily.

"Give me the phone," an authoritative female voice said. Officer Gates? Detective Reynolds. We were about to call you. Are you still with Gavin and Stacey Branch?"

"Well, that's actually what I'm calling about," he told her. "They snuck out in the middle of the night."

"Do you have any idea where they may have gone?"

"I think they're going to the Branch farm. They'd seen the case file; at the photos of Susanna Patterson's prison."

"You took the case file home and left it out?"

"It was a lapse in judgement. I take full responsibility."

"We'll deal with that later," she said. "We'll meet you at the Branch farm. I'm forwarding you a serious email. If you find the Branch's before we do, do not alert them to the content of the email, but don't let them out of your sight."

Easton felt annoyance bristling up inside him. He didn't appreciate being treated like a rookie, but it had to be tolerated when the FBI was involved.

He hung up the phone and headed to his bedroom to grab a jacket and called over his shoulder to Susanna and David. "I'll find them."

"We're coming with you," Susanna said.

"No, you're not," Easton said with finality as he pulled on his jacket.

"Of course we are!"

"No!" Easton thundered. "You aren't. Don't you get it? Until Marty and Sherry Randall are caught, you all are targets. Believe me, when I catch up to them, they're going to get chewed out too. Stop putting yourselves at risk!"

He didn't wait for her reply before grabbing his keys and running outside to his car. When his cell phone beeped, he pulled it open to read the attachment as he started the ignition.

His lungs burned when he read the content. No. There was no way this was true. He tossed his phone onto the passenger seat and turned on his siren as he tore out onto the road.

When Easton pulled up to the farmhouse, he was greeted by the flashing lights of two police cruisers.

The chief and Detective Reynolds approached him as he shot out of the car.

"Why the hell did they have the file, Gates?" the chief asked.

"We can focus on that later, gentlemen," Detective Reynolds said. "The fact of the matter is we have two high profile cases now merging together. The first order of business is to find them before something else happens."

The chief nodded and gave the order. A group of officers made their way to the opening of the secret room.

"So, you know the Branch's well?" Detective Reynolds asked him while they waited.

"Stacey better than Gavin. Our mothers are friends."

"You should have excused yourself from the case once you realized their true identities."

"I know," Easton sighed. "I did step back, but I didn't remove myself."

"What's your take on the Branch's?"

"All of them, or Stacey and Gavin?"

"Say what you need to say, Gates."

"I always found the father to be controlling and domineering, the mother too sweet. It never came off as genuine to me. Despite her relationship with my mother, I always preferred the children. I know Stacey better because they kept trying to get us to date, and we were put in situations where we'd have to interact. She's an extremely devoted, hard-working, and levelheaded person. She doesn't give up on anything. As far as Gavin goes, before I gave them a place to hide out, I could probably count my interactions with him on one hand. But he always struck me as a stand-up guy who'd walk through fire for his sister."

"Did you ever become romantically involved with Stacey?"

He flushed but answered the question honestly. "Once. When we were in California. I didn't know who she was at the time."

"But you were on an active case she was covering for her newspaper."

A group of officers exited the barn yelling all clear and made their way up to search the house instead. The chief walked back up to them, throwing his hands up in the air.

"Gates? What the hell?"

"I don't understand," Easton told him. "The file was open on the table and the photos had clearly been gone through. I thought they saw something that made them want to come back here."

"Well, they aren't there now."

"Call in an APB," Detective Reynolds told him.

"Should I say—"

"No. Let's hold onto that little nugget for now," she told him. "We may need it."

Stacey

"Stacey. Stacey!" Angie called to her.

Stacey pulled at the shower rod in the attached bathroom with all her strength, trying to get it to break loose from the wall, but it wouldn't give. She dropped to the ground and grunted in frustration.

"Come sit down," Angie told her. "There's no sense in wearing yourself out."

"I don't know how you can stand this," Stacey breathed heavily when she took a water bottle from the fridge and sat next to Angie, gulping the liquid down greedily.

"Gavin will come. He needs to calm down from everything."

Stacey gave a disbelieving laugh and shook her head. "I love my brother. God knows I do. I thought I knew him. But I don't think I could ever forgive someone who wrestles me into a hidden room and chains me to a wall."

"I didn't say anything about forgiving him," Angie said. Her face was serious and sorrowful. "But I believe I'm safe. We're safe. He'd never hurt us. Especially you. You should hear the way he talks about you. Stacey this and Stacey that. He is so proud of you."

A sudden thought came to Stacey, and she turned to her sister-in-law. "Did you lie to him about being pregnant? I mean, you said you were, but the case file says you aren't."

Angie sighed. "I thought I was. I'm six weeks late. That's not normal for me. I told him, and we did argue because he's afraid to have kids. Afraid he'll turn out like his asshole father. Then I went to the doctor, and they told me I'm not. He was at the house when I found out and I called him. We argued again because he'd already told them, and they'd all fought about it for nothing."

"That's not fair to you. Either time. I'm sorry," Stacey told her. "I don't understand what their issue with you was."

"Honestly, because I grew up rough, I think they were afraid I'd be able to see through them."

"That does make a certain amount of sense," Stacey nodded. "I don't understand why Gavin never told me."

"He wanted to protect you," Angie smiled. "You are the most important person in the world to him."

"I'm sure that's not true."

"No, really. The sun shines on you. Thank God you and I always got along because if we didn't, I promise you, I never would have had a shot in hell."

"He definitely tortured me enough as a kid."

"What big brother doesn't?"

Stacey checked her phone again, and whimpered when she saw there were no bars.

"Did you tell anyone you were coming here?"

Stacey shook her head and buried her face in her hands. "I'm an idiot."

"You wanted to protect your brother. There's nothing wrong with that. We might have to wait awhile, but he will come back. He will."

"Yeah, but those psychos are still out there." Stacey pointed toward the closed door. "What if something happens to him when he shows up?"

"Your dad—"

"That piece of shit is not my father," Stacey murmured. "He stole me and lied to me my entire life. His name is Marty Randall, and I hope they find him, and he rots in a prison cell for the rest of his life, so, he can feel even a fraction of what he put my real mother through."

"I didn't know his name," Angie said gently. "I was saying he knew Gavin knew and didn't hurt him. That's got to count for something."

Stacey snorted. "Yeah. He didn't hurt him. Just threatened to kill everyone he loved to keep him in check."

Angie hung her head, resigned.

"No," Stacey jumped to her feet again. "No. There's got to be a way out of here." She examined the door again more closely.

"Stacey, Gavin made sure there wasn't a way out of here."

"No. There's a way. Some sort of safeguard. A spring, maybe. You have to find it."

Angie readjusted her arm and hissed, screwing her face up in pain.

"You okay?" Stacey walked back over to her to examine the wounds on her wrists. The skin was raw and beginning to seep and bleed in some spots. "We have to get you out of these cuffs. That's going to get infected."

"There's nothing we can do right now."

Stacey spotted the light glinting off something in Angie's hair and ran her fingers over the spot. She pulled out a bobby pin and worked at the cuffs.

"Is that going to work?" Angie asked in disbelief.

"It's worth a try," Stacey told her. "I don't know about handcuffs, but I've picked locks with bobby pins before."

"Where the hell did you learn to do that?"

Stacey smiled. "I don't always take the most traditional steps when I'm on a story."

Ashley Bundy

She returned her gaze to the lock.

Chapter Twenty-Nine

Gavin

"I'm in deep shit," Gavin thought to himself. He sat shaking in his car, trying to figure out his next steps.

He'd been awoken by the sound of the front door closing back in Easton's apartment. He'd taken a quick sweep of the apartment and found Stacey gone. The case file sitting on the kitchen table told him everything he'd needed to know. Stacey knew. He felt sick over it.

Gavin knew for half his life he wasn't the person they were telling him to be—what they were forcing him to become. He wasn't sure he'd ever know his real identity, and he was okay with that. But he couldn't let them get away with it. He'd been planning this almost the whole time, but he'd never wanted Stacey to become involved.

His sister was the most kindhearted person he knew, and he loved that about her, but it was a curse at the same time. Stacey wouldn't care he was getting justice for what was stolen from them. She would say it was wrong. Maybe she was right. But he wanted them to burn.

Ashley Bundy

Tears streamed down his face as he thought about what must be going through her mind right now. He knew how it would look to someone who hadn't been in on the plan from the beginning. He'd panicked when he'd locked Angie up, but he hadn't hurt her. He couldn't. The plan changed, and he didn't know what to do. All he needed was time to think but everything spiraled so fast.

As he approached the yard he saw Stacey's car beyond the fence behind a bush. Then he noticed a light in the office window. He blew out his breath. Maybe she hadn't found the room yet. He may still be able to salvage this.

When Gavin walked inside the building and made his way to the office, he was surprised to see Marty and Sherry sitting on opposite sides of the desk.

"Hey there, son," Marty smirked at him and took a swig from a soda.

"Don't call me that," Gavin snarled and slammed the door shut behind him. "How the hell did you get food? Your mugs are all over the news."

Marty shrugged his shoulders. "Back door is always open at that gas station on Main. They only have one person on shift at a time. Easy enough to wait until they're distracted."

"Is there anything you won't steal?"

"A person's gotta eat. And if it weren't for you and that busy body sister of yours, we'd be able to go in and buy like normal people."

"Me and Stacey? It's our fault you had to go on the run and steal food?"

"Gavin, don't be that way, sweetie," Sherry reached out to stroke his arm, but he jerked it away from her. He momentarily felt bad when he saw the hurt on her face, but then he reminded himself she was involved in all this too.

"Damn right," Marty pressed on. "We were doing fine until you two got old enough to start being defiant. How many times did we try to get it through your thick skulls to mind your own business? But no, you were always going around looking in rooms you had no business being in. And your sister taking that reporter job. Being paid to be nosy."

"Well, I'm so sorry we made it hard for you to be crooks."

"Don't you sass me, boy," Marty growled. "You might not like it, but we saved you from that woman. She was a lousy mother,"

"How can you possibly know that? Because she broke down on the side of the road? That happens to everyone at some point."

"A good mother wouldn't have you out in the middle of the night in that weather, anyway. A good mother would have you snuggled up in warm beds where you belonged."

"Who made you judge and jury?" Gavin slammed his hands down on the desk in front of Marty, then swept his sandwich onto the floor.

Marty jumped to his feet and Sherry grabbed Gavin to pull him behind her. She placed a hand on each of the men's chests, keeping them apart.

"Stop! Stop! Please. It doesn't matter how we came together, we're still family."

"You're no family of mine." Gavin pulled her hand from his chest and stared straight into her eyes. "You're only marginally better than him. The only family I have left I can trust is Stacey."

Marty laughed. "Her? Don't think for one second, she won't throw you under the bus for a big story. She did it to us. She'll do it to you."

"What are you even doing here?"

"No one works on the weekends. You have that cot in the back. We're going to stay here until tomorrow night when you are going to lend us one of these vehicles and give us some money to get by on for a while."

"Why the hell would I give you anything?"

"Because you owe us. And if you don't and we get caught we'll spill your little secret. How do you think the world would feel if they knew your old man helped you build your little torture chamber?"

Sherry's eyes went wide in shock. "Gavin?"

Gavin continued to stare Marty down. "I fucking hate you."

Marty grinned. "I know. Now, go get us some real food."

There was a mechanical sound coming from the other room and Gavin's heart raced. He swung out and punched Marty in the jaw, knocking him backward where he fell and hit his head on the corner of the desk.

Sherry gasped and put her hands up to her mouth. "What did you do?" she screamed.

Gavin grabbed the keys off the desk and shoved her toward Marty before backing out of the room and locking the door.

He rounded the corner and narrowly missed the tire iron swinging at his head.

"Gavin?" Stacey yelled in surprise. She stood there with a wide stance, hair in disarray and holding the tire iron in front of her like a bat. Angie stood a couple of feet behind her massaging her wrists. "What are you doing here?"

"I came looking for you. Come on. We gotta go. I locked them in there."

There was a scream of rage and a pounding noise coming from behind him. "Come on!" He grabbed the girls and pulled them toward the front door.

CHAPTER THIRTY

Stacey headed in the direction of the passenger seat of Gavin's car.

"No!" he grabbed her and pulled her and Angie toward the bushes. "We have to take your car. They won't expect it. They don't know you're here."

"Sherry does."

Stacey told him about Sherry closing the door on her, locking her in with Angie.

"She doesn't want to hurt us," Gavin said, checking the rear window. "She had an opportunity with both of us and didn't take it. She'll stall him, but we need to go somewhere safe."

"Where?"

"The farmhouse. Take us to the farmhouse. With the way the police have been nosing around lately it',ll be the last place they'll look for us."

Stacey was glad to see the red and blue lights cutting through the night sky when she pulled in front of the farmhouse. Gavin told her to pull into the woods, but she'd refused. She was done listening to him until she got some answers.

Easton walked out of the barn, threw up his arms, and mouthed "What the fuck?" at her. Officers were swarming everywhere, and many already had their hands on their weapons.

The three passengers got out of the car with their hands up, and Easton gave the call to stand down as he approached them. He told the officer nearest him to go get Detective Reynolds from the house. His eyes went wide when he saw Angie standing there.

"What the hell is going on?" He asked them.

Stacey launched into the story of how she'd found Angie in the secret room and Gavin followed her and locked Marty and Sherry in the office.

"Are they still there?" Easton asked.

"Probably not. That lock is flimsy, and he threw his full weight into the door when we ran out of there."

Detective Reynolds ran across the grass toward them. "Are you all okay?" She asked. Then her eyes landed on Angie. "Angie Branch?"

Easton quickly told the detective what the group told him, and she ordered a nearby group of officers to go to the auto shop at once.

Easton's eyes were narrowed on Gavin and Stacey like daggers. "You two were reckless tonight," he admonished. "If something came to you, Stacey, you should have woken me up. Gavin, I'm not going to ask what the hell such a room is doing in your shop right now, but you sure as hell better believe we will be talking about that later."

He then turned toward Angie and his expression softened. "I'm glad you're okay, however, one of my officers has already called for an ambulance."

Angie shook her head and waved her arms slightly. "Oh, no. That's okay. I'm fine. I don't need all that."

"It's standard procedure," he told her. "We have to make sure your wounds aren't infected. Once you're cleared, I'll need you to come down to the station to give your statement."

Stacey didn't miss the glance that passed between Gavin and Angie. She tutted around until the ambulance pulled in and took Angie and Gavin toward the hospital. Then she let out an audible sigh when they were gone.

"You have anything else to tell me?" Easton asked. His tone was hard as steel, and he had his arms crossed in front of him.

"I don't know," she answered honestly and pulled her sweater tightly around her before wandering back toward her car.

"Damn it, Stacey," he snarled as he followed her. He gently grabbed her arm and pulled her back. "If you know something and aren't telling me, you're impeding this investigation."

"Officer Gates, take your hands off her," Detective Reynolds said, and he removed his hand, but he didn't back away.

"My whole world is shattering around me right now, Easton," she told him. "I don't know what to think of it. I don't know what's real and what's only a theory. If I shared every thought that crossed my mind, I'd never be taken seriously."

"I can't even imagine what you're going through right now. But we are never going to be able to get to the bottom of this if you're keeping things from me. I need you to tell me the truth. Did Gavin have something to do with what happened here tonight?"

Stacey looked at them with tortured eyes. The woman gave her a reassuring smile and shook her head. Stacey sighed. "Angie said he put her in the room but swears he didn't hurt her. And he did lock Marty and Sherry in the office so we could escape."

Easton nodded. "Okay. How the hell did he even know about that room?"

"He built it." Her voice cracked on the statement and tears streamed down her face. He pulled her into his arms and whispered that everything would be okay as he stroked her hair.

Chapter Thirty-One

When Stacey and Easton entered Angie's room in the ER, the doctor was finishing up wrapping her wrists.

Stacey went over and hugged her. "How's it going?"

"Doc says I have a minor infection. He's giving me a script for antibiotics and painkillers. I can leave soon though."

"You got out in time," the doctor told her. "Another day or two it could have gotten bad. I'll go get those prescriptions for you and start your discharge paperwork."

"Where's Gavin?" Stacey asked as the doctor walked out of the room.

"He went to the vending machine." Angie narrowed her eyebrows. "He should be back by now."

Stacey and Easton shared a glance over her head.

"When did he leave?" Easton asked.

"God, I'm not sure. It was before the doctor came in to dress my wounds. Tracking time has gotten weird the past few days."

Easton pulled out his radio. "Call to all units. Need a sweep of St. Lucy's Hospital. Watch all exit points. Find Gavin Branch."

"No, no," Angie's eyes went wide. "Really. He went to the vending machine to get me something to eat."

"You said it yourself," Easton said gently. "He should be back by now."

An hour later, Stacey and Angie were sitting together in an interrogation room at the station holding hands. The officers hadn't found Gavin, despite checking the hospital.

They jumped when Detective Reynolds entered the room and shut the door behind her. She gave them a wide smile before taking her seat. "Hi, ladies. Thank you for your patience."

"Where's Easton?" Stacey asked.

"It would be inappropriate for Officer Gates to be her for this part, considering his personal involvement."

Stacey's mouth was so dry when she swallowed that she felt like rocks were tearing at her throat. She hoped Easton wasn't in trouble. She'd never forgive herself if he lost his job because of her.

"Mrs. Branch, do you have any idea where your husband may have gone?" Detective Reynolds asked, turning to Angie.

Angie shook her head, and a single tear rolled down her cheek. "I can't believe he left me there."

Stacey squeezed her hand.

"But you were able to believe it when he locked you in the room at his shop?"

"He didn't hurt me. He was upset."

Detective Reynolds watched them both sympathetically and then leaned forward on the desk. "Sometimes the people we love the most hurt us the most. We'll tolerate more from them. We see their good qualities."

"I don't understand," Angie insisted. "Why would he leave me at the hospital like that? That's not Gavin."

The detective took a deep breath before speaking. Stacey felt the thinness in the room, as if the atmosphere tried to mentally prepare her for the blow that was about to come.

"I have something to share with you ladies that you aren't going to like. It's most likely going to shock you, but things are going to be public come morning, and I don't want you to have to hear this somewhere else."

Stacey and Angie squeezed hands before Stacey nodded at the detective to continue.

"We received a flag in the database today. Gavin's DNA was a match to the scene at Lauren Schiff's residence."

"Who is that?" Angie asked.

"You ladies know about the missing girls last year?"

They nodded.

"Lauren was one of the victims."

"I thought there was no DNA," Stacey said. "That's what was so scary. Nothing was left behind at any of the scenes."

Detective Reynolds nodded. "That is what was publicly released. There was blood found in Lauren's bedroom that did not match her. The information was kept internal as leverage. For months there were no matches. But once Gavin's DNA was entered into the system, we got our match."

Nausea rolled in Stacey's stomach, clenching her gut.

"I don't understand," Angie said, her eyes furrowed.

"Either he was romantically involved with her, or he had something to do with her disappearance. Which would mean he was probably involved with the others, as well."

Stacey shot from her seat to hover over the trash can in the corner until the contents of her stomach emptied.

"Are you okay, Stacey?" Detective Reynolds put a comforting hand on her back.

She stood there for a moment, doubled over. Once she was sure she was done, she straightened up, nodded her head, and wiped her mouth.

"Do you need to take a break?"

Stacey shook her head. "No. No, let's do this."

She returned to her seat and looked over at Angie, who was bright red. "Are you saying my husband is a murderer?"

Detective Reynolds sat down and chose her next words carefully. "We don't know that. No bodies have been found. But there is sufficient evidence he was behind the disappearances. He may be holding them somewhere. I should tell you that the secret room in his auto shop had DNA evidence in it of at least two of the missing girls. We believe he held them there at some point, then moved them."

"No." Angie shook her head. "If he was kidnapping women and keeping them there, he never would have told me about the room. He said we were going to capture Marty and Sherry and put them in there so we could all safely get away."

"Did he volunteer that information openly," Detective Reynolds said softly, "or did you walk in on him building it and that was the excuse he gave?"

Angie hung her head as the tears flowed down her cheeks.

"Does he have any more rooms like that? Any places he spends an unusual amount of time?"

Stacey couldn't think of a single place that would seem unnatural or unusual. She believed Angie didn't know anything either, by the way she shook her head.

"Alright, ladies," Detective Reynolds sighed and sat back. "I trust you'll call me if you think of anything."

Carmen Reynolds

When she walked into the interrogation room the following morning, she was ready to nail someone to a wall. Lack of sleep did nothing to deter her; if anything, it drove her and made her more alert. She always did best on the cases she got the last amount of sleep on.

Henry Rusher was seated at the table next to his attorney, with disheveled hair, a wrinkled jumpsuit, and red-rimmed eyes. He appeared like he'd been tortured the whole night. Good. She wasn't at all sorry to bring the cocky son of a bitch off his pedestal.

"Detective," Attorney Alden Swift said coolly as he stared her down. "We're ready to see what grounds you have to hold my client."

"Gladly," she said as she took her seat. "I will start with the Patterson case. We have evidence to suggest Mr. Rusher took a company expense paid trip to California in '98 to speak to Sherry Randall's sister, Priscilla. Priscilla passed not long after, but her husband Jerry confirmed this visit with us. He said they were directed to the home of Sherry and Marty Randall."

Rusher huffed and crossed his arms over his chest. Detective Reynolds chose to ignore him and continue.

"During that same trip he paid for false identities for two adults and two children. That informant has come forward as well. The purchase has been verified, and those identities have been confirmed to be for Alice, Paul, Stacey, and Gavin Branch, respectively."

Attorney Swift didn't speak but stared over at Rusher with wide eyes.

"Additionally, we have found something else rather disturbing regarding this case. It turns out former detective Rusher's daughter is none other than Tia Ross Patterson. A member of our office did go to the Patterson home to bring Tia in for questioning, but she was not home. After tracing her credit card we saw that she purchased a plane ticket here. We're presuming to be with her husband during this difficult time. She's due to land later today, and she will be met at the airport at that time."

"You can't trace her credit cards!" Rusher said furiously.

"Actually, we can. A judge signed off on a warrant. Now, I don't know exactly what your motive was with this, but I have a pretty good idea. Your daughter was sleeping with a rich, affluential man, and when his wife and kids went missing you saw a golden opportunity for her to swoop in and get it all."

"Detective," Swift said sharply.

"All that is bad enough," Detective Reynolds continued, "but that is not where the misconduct ends. See, this prompted a thorough investigation of all cases where you were the lead investigator. That perfectly solved case streak seemed suspicious in light of everything else. At latest count, there were fifteen mismanaged cases that were clearly not investigated."

She slid a printout across the table to Attorney Swift. "All of these cases have been reopened, and our FBI field office is still sifting through records. If there are more indiscretions, I assure you we will find them. Now, Mr. Swift, I will leave you to confer with your client."

Detective Reynolds rose from her chair and exit the room, making her way down the long hallway until she reached the lobby. She saw David and Susanna Patterson sitting in chairs along one wall.

David immediately shot to his feet when he saw her and extended his hand. "Detective Reynold. How are you doing? I received a message there was a development in the case?"

"Yes. I'll need to speak to you for a moment."

"Of course. Anything you need."

"Do you need me too?" Susanna asked.

"I will need to speak to you, if you'll hold tight, please. I need to talk to David about a different aspect of the case. If you'll follow me, please."

She led David to the chief's office instead of one of the interrogation rooms. There was no need to make him uncomfortable. He wasn't a suspect.

"Is this regarding my son?" David asked as he took a seat on the opposite side of the desk.

"No, why? Has he contacted you?"

He shook his head. "No. But I'll admit I'm concerned after he took off the way he did."

"No, I wanted to talk to you about something else that came up in our investigation. Can you tell me about the detective you originally spoke to when you first reported Susanna missing? Was he helpful and friendly to you?"

"At first, he was kind and reassuring. I mean he had a no-nonsense attitude, and I knew I was a suspect as the spouse, but he was perfectly professional. But then—"

"Then what, Mr. Patterson?"

"He seemed to change for no reason. After I got that phone call from Susanna, and he came out here, it was like dealing with an entirely different person. I was no longer a suspect, but he didn't seem to care about the truth at all. Told me some women are vindictive and will go to extreme lengths to get back at their partners for an affair. It didn't matter how many people told him that's not the kind of person Susanna was, he didn't want to hear it."

"Okay. Can we fast forward a bit to your life in the aftermath? I understand you remarried."

"Yes."

"And that marriage is to Tia Ross, am I correct? Wasn't she the same woman you admitted to having the affair with?"

David hung his head.

"I'm not judging you, Mr. Patterson. I do need to have a thorough understanding of the situation."

"Yes," his voice was hoarse as he forced out the word. "It was Tia. She was my secretary at the bank."

"Was this a prolonged relationship or a single encounter?"

David sighed. "Both. We'd developed a flirty relationship a couple of months before and gone to lunch together a few times. That was the first time it was physical. And that was completely on me. Susanna and I were having problems. That was the day of the week she normally took the kids to the park with other moms and kids. Kind of a mommy and me thing, I guess.

"Tia pushed me to take our relationship to the next level for a couple of weeks, but I refused to do it at the office. It seemed unprofessional to me, so we went back to the house during my lunch. Susanna came home and found us."

"And you continued this relationship even after your wife and children went missing, and you were pleading in the news for them to return?"

"Not at first," he protested. "I was so overcome with guilt in the beginning I cut things off, and she said she understood. I talked to her about concerns and fears about a year later, and we slowly rekindled things."

"So, the two of you married in '98?"

"'99."

"And you have a child together?"

"We have a fifteen-year-old son. Jake. I'm sorry. I'm not trying to be argumentative here. I'm genuinely confused. Why are you asking me about my wife and son? How is it relevant to what's happening now?"

"Puzzle pieces, Mr. Patterson." She smiled at him. "What about your wife's family? Did you ever meet them?"

"I met an aunt and some cousins. Her mother died before we met, and she didn't have a relationship with her father. He was almost entirely absent when she was a child. Left her mom for another woman when she was young."

Detective Reynolds nodded. "Yes, that tracks with what we have. I'm going to be real with you here, and you may be shocked by what I'm about to tell you. Your wife's father is Henry Rusher, the lead investigator on Susanna's case."

David's jaw dropped. "What? How is that even possible?"

"We don't know the extent of her knowledge on this. She may not have even known he was involved in the case. They did have an estranged relationship when she was a minor. Whether or not they developed a relationship after she turned eighteen, we don't know. If you were never introduced to him, chances are they didn't. But we do need to speak to her. Another agent went to your home in Boston and found she wasn't there. Credit card records show she's actually on her way here right now. Did you know she was coming?"

David shook his head. "No. She didn't even want me to come out here. We fought about it. I'm surprised she's coming."

"Like I said, she could be unaware of her father's actions. We ask you don't speak to her until we get a chance to speak to her. An officer will be meeting her at the airport."

He nodded, and she felt sympathy. "Could you send Susanna in, please?"

"Of course," he said and swiftly left the room.

Detective Reynolds checked her email for a moment before the door reopened and Susanna stuck her head inside.

"Susanna," Detective Reynolds smiled. "Please come in. Take a seat."

Susanna came in and took a seat tentatively. Detective Reynolds took a moment to take in her appearance. The woman seemed better than she had a couple of days before but was still in rough shape. She was much too thin and pale, though her eyes were brighter.

"How are you adjusting?"

Susanna brought her knees up to her chest. "Is it weird I can't get used to sleeping in a bed?"

"I think that's normal after so long of sleeping sitting up."

Susanna sighed and stared straight into Detective Reynold's eyes. "Can you give it to me straight, Detective? My son is running because he's got something to do with those missing girls, doesn't he?"

"Have I been that transparent?"

"I was worried about this. All those years down in that dark, dingy room. You have nothing to do but think in a situation like that. I thought about my children being brought up by that man and I feared how they might turn out."

"Did you ever see or hear anything that might indicate if he had somewhere else to hide?"

Susanna shook her head. "Marty was careful about what he said in front of me regarding the children. Usually, it was taunts about how much better off they were without me, but no specifics. No names or hobbies or anything like that. Once, when he was keeping me in the barn, before the room, I thought I saw him peek in. Of course, I tried to convince myself it wasn't him. He didn't rush into my defense or anything. I'm still not even sure he actually saw me. When David and I met him that first time, he said he saw me in the barn once, and he was sent away. It still doesn't explain why he didn't react to seeing something like that."

"I don't want to fill you with false hope, Susanna," Detective Reynolds said gently. "I'd love to tell you Gavin might not be responsible, but I can't do that. We found his blood at one of the crime scenes, and he's guilty of locking his own wife up in a similar room to yours. By her own admission."

"Officer Gates said that." Susanna nodded in agreement. "But I don't understand. Even if he's responsible for those other women, why would he lock up his own wife?"

"Well, we didn't get a chance to ask him," Detective Reynolds told her. "But from what we can gather, there was a disagreement about her releasing you."

Susanna let out a strangled sob.

"I'm sorry," Detective Reynolds said. "I can't even imagine how difficult this must be for you. I wish I didn't have to tell you these things. But I believe it's better to be honest than to let you hear in the news."

"Thank you. I appreciate that," Susanna wiped a tear from her cheek.

"Do you want to continue the interview, or do you need a minute?"

"I can continue. Please go on."

"We all know you were kept in the barn, and then under it at the house here. When you all were in California, where were you kept? That was an ordinary house in an ordinary neighborhood."

"There was a converted garage."

"Neighbors didn't hear any sounds?"

"He said it was soundproofed. I don't know if that was the truth or not. But as far as I know, no one came asking questions. The windows were blacked out so no one could see in. Honestly, that wasn't as bad. It was well insulated, so I didn't feel the elements much and I had more room to move."

"He didn't chain you to the wall?"

"There was a chain, but it was long, so I could walk around a bit as long as I didn't try to go too far. A couple of feet at least. Then one day Marty came out in the middle of the night and said we had to leave. Stuffed a gag in my mouth, threw me over his shoulder and chained me into the back of his truck. I could smell smoke. He must have drugged me. The next thing I knew, it was the barn. The barn was miserable. Unbelievably cold in the winter, hot as blazes in the summer. And no length in my chain so I stayed on the wall."

"What about food and clothing? Medical care?"

"Sherry was good about food for a while. She'd bring it to me a couple of times a day, and he didn't stop her. Decent quality meals too. Eventually, it stopped. I was never told why. I don't know if it was a punishment over something I did, or they simply couldn't afford it."

"They stopped feeding you?"

"Not altogether. They'd bring me something about three times a week, I guess. Usually something that was on the verge of spoiling or scraps from the bottom of a pot. They were better with water. I got a bottle of water a day. I learned to savor it.

"I was only ever provided with clothing if something literally happened to whatever I was already wearing."

"Such as?"

"One time, Marty whipped me so hard my shirt tore, and I heavily bled. It was a tattered rag. I was later brought an old nightgown of Sherry's. She's a lot bigger than me, so it hung on me, but it was better than nothing."

"What about medical care? It sounds like you suffered some pretty egregious injuries at their hands. Did you ever get sick?"

"Sherry would treat open wounds. She did it in secret at first. She'd come out in the middle of the night and put salve on the cuts. When Marty found out he was mad, but she managed to convince him if I got an infection or bled to death, it would be bad for them, so he eventually allowed it. Broken bones were never treated. I know I had broken ribs and a thumb for sure over the years.

"One winter, I'm almost positive I got pneumonia. I was struggling to breathe and had a fever. Marty gave me an inhaler. No clue where he got it. It would help in the moment, but I still struggle to take deep breaths now."

"Can you tell me what happened here?" Detective Reynolds gestured toward her cheek, and Susanna's hand flew to the scar.

"Marty. I don't even remember what I supposedly did. I think he was drunk that night. He came in yelling and put a knife to my face. Said he was going to cut out my eye if I didn't tell him what he wanted to know. I didn't know the answer. He was about to do it, but Sherry grabbed his arm, and he got my cheek instead. Sherry got him out of there, came back in, apologized for his behavior, and sewed me up the best she could."

The chief stuck his head in the room. "Detective Reynolds, I'm sorry to interrupt. Officer Jenkins came in with Tia Patterson. I put them in interrogation room C."

"Thank you, Chief," she gave him an appreciative smile. "We're finishing up." She turned back to Susanna and didn't miss the sorrow on her face.

"I'm sorry," she told her. "I know this is probably painful for you. I'll do my best to make sure you're not in the same room as her."

Susanna nodded but didn't say anything.

"How are you and David getting along?"

Susanna sighed. "It's awkward, but we haven't fought at all. We haven't discussed what happened between us yet. It's all been about what we can do to help our kids and what happened while I was away. I'm sure that conversation is coming. Especially with *her* here now."

"Did Officer Gates bring you in this morning?"

"Yes."

"Be sure to tell him to go ahead and take you away while I'm talking to Mrs. Patterson."

"What about David?"

"I'm sure he'll probably want to see his wife. If he chooses to stay, we'll have someone drive him."

Susanna nodded before rising to her feet and exiting the room.

Detective Reynolds finished typing up a few notes on the computer and made her way to interrogation room C.

The woman pacing the room was clearly high society. She wore a figure-hugging blue dress and high heels and sported perfect hair and makeup.

"Where is my husband?" she demanded the moment, the door opened.

"Good morning, Mrs. Patterson," Detective Reynolds said as she made her way to a chair. "Have a seat."

"I asked you a question. Where is my husband?"

"Take a seat," Detective Reynolds repeated, more harshly this time.

Her tone must have spoken volumes because Tia pursed her lips and slammed down into the chair opposite the detective.

"I'm Detective Carmen Reynolds with the FBI."

"What do you want with me?"

"We need to ask you a few questions. The missing person's case regarding your husband's first wife and children has been officially reopened."

"What's that got to do with me?"

"Your name has popped up a lot."

"Am I under arrest?"

"Not at this time. No. We do, however, need to talk to you to get a better understanding of the full picture."

"Can I have an attorney?"

"You can have one if you want. Your father's attorney is probably still here. I can go ask him for a referral, if you like."

"Wait a minute," Tia waved her hands in front of her face as her haughty disposition was replaced with confusion. "My father? What are you talking about? I haven't seen my father since I was twelve years old."

"It turns out he covered the whereabouts and identities of the kidnappers."

"Okay. Back up and tell me the whole story."

CHAPTER THIRTY-THREE

"Please stop pacing. You're making me nervous." Stacey smiled at Susanna to show she meant no malice with her request.

Angie sat in a chair near the window staring out.

Accommodation was made to move everyone to a motel. They couldn't all stay in Easton's apartment.

Susanna stopped pacing. She removed her hand from her mouth where she'd bitten her fingernail into the quick.

"I'm sorry. I didn't even realize I was doing it." She sank down on the end of one of the beds. She hadn't been doing it well. Susanna still walked with a limp and shook when she stood for too long, but it was getting better every day.

"It's okay," Stacey reassured her. "You spent so long not being able to move. Your body probably does it on autopilot." She looked over at her sister-in-law who barely spoke anymore. "You okay, Ang?"

Angie nodded then checked her phone again.

"You still haven't heard from him?"

"I can't believe he left me like that," she said dejectedly. "I don't want to believe what Detective Reynolds said, but why else would he run off like that? After all we've been through."

"Does he treat you well?" Susanna asked. "I mean, is he a good husband?"

Angie stared at her for a moment before answering. "Yeah, he's the best. He's the only reason I have any self-confidence at all."

Susanna strode over to the other side of the bed to sit and take Angie's hand in hers. "I don't know why his blood was at that crime scene. I don't know the extent of his involvement with those missing girls. But no one knows him better than you. If he is good to you and has a good heart, then you hold on to that. No matter what his involvement is, it doesn't change the growth you have experienced. I don't want to see you disappear down a dark hole. Keep your head high, baby girl."

Stacey noticed a rapport between Susanna and Angie. They got along from their first meeting, and it felt natural. Her own interactions with Susanna had been awkward at best, and she couldn't help but find it a bit odd. One thing that did surprise her was the fact that she didn't feel any jealousy.

She was about to make a supportive comment when her phone chirped. She checked the screen and her blood ran cold.

A picture of Beth filled her screen. She was gagged and mascara ran down her tear-streaked face. The caption under the picture read, *Meet me at the farmhouse. No police.* She flicked her eyes up to the number and saw it was sent from Gavin. Her brother had officially lost his mind.

"Guys. We have a problem."

Susanna and Angie walked over to glance over her shoulder. Susanna's hand flew to her mouth, and a tear fell down Angie's face.

"Let's go," Stacey said, and grabbed her keys.

"What has this monster done to him?" Susanna murmured from the backseat.

Stacey sped as fast as she dared down Route 6. She tossed her phone to Angie and told her to call Easton.

"No!" Angie exclaimed and dropped the phone into the center console like a hot potato. "He said no police!"

Stacey didn't stress this. She'd already discreetly dropped her location and sent it to Easton. She hoped he'd see it in time, or she'd be able to get through to Gavin.

Stacey took the few minutes left in the drive to try and get in Gavin's head. She liked to think she knew him better than anyone. Why Beth? Why did he grab her? It was obvious he knew she'd come. He'd never hurt Beth. They'd known each other since they were children, and he'd even had a crush on her once upon a time. This was a bluff. It had to be.

When she pulled into the drive for the farmhouse, she pulled up behind a car she didn't recognize and searched for any sign of life.

The farm was eerily quiet. The wind didn't move through the trees, the animals didn't make noise, crickets didn't chirp in the grass. The hair on the back of her neck stood on end at the unnaturalness of it.

"Why is it so quiet?" Susanna asked, echoing her thoughts and giving her momentary relief.

That's when it finally hit her. It wasn't just quiet. The farm was usually quiet at night. It was more so the stillness and heaviness in the air. Oppressive pressure sat on her shoulders like a weight. It occurred to her they might even be going to war.

"Give me a minute," she said before she laid her head against the headrest and squeezed her eyes tight.

"Come on. Come on," she willed an image to come forward and guide her, but nothing was happening. She grunted and slapped the wheel before throwing her head back against the headrest.

It was so frustrating she'd get random flashes when she wasn't trying, but when she actually needed it, she couldn't figure out how to use the ability.

"Don't shut it out," a voice spoke softly in her head. *"Let it in!"*

"I'm trying!" Stacey screeched.

"Trying what?" Angie asked her and wrinkled her forehead.

Susanna squeezed her shoulders, and Stacey felt calmness flood throughout her body. Her heartrate slowed and her breathing evened.

"Let it in, baby," Susanna whispered.

Stacey didn't have a chance to respond before the fog surrounded her, and she flipped and twisted through open space before she saw a dark room with a dirt floor where Beth sat on the ground, crying. The vision didn't show her Gavin's location, and that concerned her, but she couldn't dwell on it too long.

She came back to herself and gestured to the glove box. "There's a flashlight in there. Why don't you get that out?"

Angie dug to the bottom and pulled out a flashlight.

"We need to get to the barn," Stacey told them.

"How do you know—" Angie asked as she handed her the flashlight. Susanna interrupted.

"She knows."

Stacey glanced into the rearview mirror and met Susanna's gaze. The woman gave her a reassuring smile and nodded her head. How did she know about Stacey's ability? Was it a motherly instinct? Could she do it herself? There were so many questions, so much to talk about when this night was over, but they had to get through it first.

She pulled the keys from the ignition and looked over Susanna's shoulder, to see police lights. She didn't want them to deal with this on their own, but it appeared they had no choice.

She took a deep breath and got out of the car followed by the other women. The night air was filled with a chill that was unnatural for that time of year. The wind blew harshly, whipping Stacey's hair into her face.

As a unit, the women approached the barn. As they walked up, she saw Susanna shaking next to her and grabbed the woman's hand. Stacey didn't know if she'd ever be able to view

Susanna as her mother, but she had immense respect for this woman, who cared enough about them to walk back toward her prison, despite being terrified.

Once inside, they made their way to the hole in the ground at the edge of the barn. Stacey's breath caught in her throat. She couldn't imagine how this wasn't noticeable to her before. Sure, she'd been told to stay out of the barn, but she'd spent her share of time sneaking in; she'd never been caught like Gavin.

Her father's workbench was slid over the opening, but it still should have been obvious. There were deep gouges in the earth to indicate something heavy regularly got moved.

She made her way toward the hole when a bright light illuminated the room.

"Stop right there," Gavin ordered as he stepped out of the shadows. He'd lost five pounds since she'd seen him last, his skin was pale, and his hair was ruffled, going every which way.

His face was set with a hard edge and there was a coldness in his eyes that scared her. She'd never seen her brother look so wild. He turned toward Susanna and Angie standing behind her.

"I said come alone," he said.

"You said no police," she countered. "Do you see a police officer?"

"Gavin, baby," Angie walked toward him, and he put up a hand.

"Stop. Step back. Don't come near me."

"We're here, Gavin," Stacey fought to keep the quaver out of her voice. *Don't show fear. Don't let it in*, she said to herself. "Is Beth alive?"

"What do you take me for?" he snarled. There was a dangerous flash in his eyes, but she would not give him the satisfaction of reacting.

"I don't know, Gavin. What should I take you for? Your actions aren't those of an innocent person. You sent me a picture of her tied up and crying. What am I supposed to think?"

"Everything I've ever done; I've done for you. All of you." He took a step forward and jabbed a finger in their direction.

"You kidnapped women for me?" she spat, stepping toward him as the anger flooded over her. "That's rich."

"I didn't kill anyone!" He yelled. "Those girls are safe!"

"Well, they weren't in your little torture room. Where the hell are they then?"

"Stacey," Susanna whispered, and walked up behind her to gently grip her shoulders in warning.

"You," he spat and stared at Susanna. "Do you have any idea what you've done?"

"I haven't done anything," Susanna said coolly, but her nails dug into Stacey's shoulders.

He laughed. "This whole thing was your idea."

Stacey stepped to the side to see Susanna's face, but the woman seemed as confused as she was. Her mouth hung open, and her eyebrows were furrowed. "I never suggested you hurt anyone."

Gavin pointed at her and stared into Stacey's eyes once again. "She said we needed to give him a dose of his own medicine. She said if the cops wouldn't investigate us, we would need to blame him for something else."

"Wait a minute," Stacey looked between the two of them. "Did you two speak? Before your escape? Why didn't you say anything before?"

"I didn't want him to get in trouble," Susanna's voice squeaked.

"You told him to kidnap girls?"

"No!" Susanna exclaimed and grabbed her arms. "I did say Marty would probably have to be caught for something else before we could get justice, but I never instructed your brother to do anything to anyone. I only meant I doubted this was the man's only crime."

"I knew what you wanted." Gavin shook his head. He now had a nerve-wracking wildness in his features and Stacey placed her body in front of Susanna's.

"Back up against the wall." Stacey jumped at the sound of the voice coming from the other side of the barn. Angie stood there with a wide stance, a handgun held firmly in both her hands, and it was pointed at Gavin.

Stacey had forgotten Angie was there. It had been a long while since she'd said anything, and it appeared Gavin forgot about her too.

"Hey, babe. What are you doing?"

"You lied to me! You never said anything about kidnapping women to frame him. I wouldn't have helped you. You said we were going to lock him in and free her."

"Put the gun down, Angie," he said coldly. "You're not going to use it. You're embarrassing yourself."

"Do you not see you're talking like him?" She shook her head as the tears flowed down her face. "You've turned into him."

Gavin ran at Angie full force, and Susanna grabbed Stacey's arm, roughly pulling her from the barn as the gun went off.

Stacey couldn't bring herself to turn around. The two of them ran as fast as they could toward the house and burst in through the front door. Stacey immediately slammed the door behind them and pushed a table in front of the door.

"STACEY!!!" Gavin screamed wildly from outside.

"What do we do?" Susanna asked.

Stacey's eyes shot to every corner of the room as she tried to think.

"Back door!" she hissed and grabbed the other woman's arm to lead her to the kitchen. She gasped when they entered the room to find Gavin leaning against the doorjamb to the back door, blocking their exit.

"Hey, sis," he said softly. The moonlight shown through the open door behind Gavin, casting him in a menacing glow.

"Gavin," she squeaked. "You don't need to do this. We can talk. We've always been able to talk, right?"

He walked inside, slammed the door, and effortlessly pushed the ancient china cabinet in front of the door. He then took another step toward her.

Susanna threw herself in front of Stacey. "Your sister has done nothing wrong. Calm down!"

He growled and ran toward them, grabbed Susanna by the shoulders and tossed her aside. "Don't tell me what to do! I'm tired of everyone telling me what to do!"

Gavin pushed Stacey against the wall and wrapped his hands around her throat. His eyes were wild as he stared into hers.

Stacey fought to pry his hands away from her throat, but it was like trying to get a bone away from a dog. The air began to thin, and tears streamed down her face.

"Why couldn't you believe in me?" he asked her quietly. The softness in his voice was almost as terrifying as what he was doing to her. "Why couldn't anyone believe in me?"

Darkness loomed around the edges of her vision. *"This is it,"* she thought to herself.

A loud crash echoed throughout the otherwise quiet room, and Gavin crumpled to the ground. Susanna stood behind him with a frying pan. She dropped it and stared at her hand as if she couldn't believe what she'd done.

Stacey coughed and clutched her throat.

"Are you okay?" Susanna asked her.

Stacey nodded and allowed the tears to flow down her face.

Gavin groaned and began to pull himself up from the floor.

"How?" Susanna exclaimed.

Stacey grabbed an oil lamp off the counter in one hand and Susanna's hand with the other. They ran for the stairs and toward Stacey's old bedroom as Gavin's yells followed them.

They shoved a bookshelf in front of the door as they heard splintering crashes grew closer.

"What are we doing?" Susanna asked as she looked around.

"Improvising," Stacey whispered. She strode to the window to look out and gauge their distance to the ground.

Gavin began banging on her door. The bookcase would slow him down, but it wouldn't keep him out forever. They had to move.

She grabbed a cannister of kerosene for the lamp in her bedroom and began to toss it over every surface. Susanna caught on and did the same with her lamp.

The wood of the door splintered, and Gavin's arm slid through a hole, feeling for the shelf to push it away.

Stacey climbed out of her window and onto the roof, eyeing a tree a few feet away. She prayed they'd be able to reach it. She helped Susanna out onto the roof, and they carefully slid in the direction of the tree.

Stacey took a great leap and grabbed hold of a branch, swinging onto it and settling it between her legs. She reached out to grab Susanna's hand and pull her onto the branch as well. She fumbled in her pocket for the book of matches, struck one, and tossed it in the window.

The house lit up like a Christmas tree. The fire spread quickly and high as mother and daughter shimmied their way down the trunk of the tree and ran in the opposite direction.

"Where did this wind come from?" Susanna yelled as they ran, and a bad feeling punched Stacey square in the gut.

Stacey turned around and felt the violent breeze before she saw the sparks from the house blowing in the wind and landing on the roof of the barn.

"Oh my God! Angie and Beth!"

They ran full force to the barn.

"You get Angie!" Stacey yelled as she ran toward the dark hole. "I'll get Beth!"

She made her way into the dark room, which was filled with smoke, but no actual flames yet. With no light to guide her, she followed muffled screams before she came to Beth. She was on her knees on the ground with her arm chained to the wall.

Stacey pulled the gag from Beth's mouth, and she tried to pull in deep breaths, but instead coughed on the deep smoke. Stacey pulled her shirt up over her nose and mouth and then grabbed the chain and shook it, hoping to free her friend, but it held tight.

"Let it in," the voice said in her head before an image of a key filled her mind. She looked toward the spot her vision showed her and felt until she found it. She quickly opened the lock.

Stacey and Beth dove for the hole, climbing their way into the fire-filled barn. Stacey heard the splintering sound of a collapsing beam before she saw it. She pushed Beth forward seconds before it would have hit her. Stacey jumped over the beam and yelled at Beth to get out of the barn.

She looked around frantically for any sign of movement. She had to make sure Susanna and Angie got out safely, or she would never be able to forgive herself. Then she saw them.

Susanna was on her knees beating at flames that crept up Angie's legs. Stacey raced forward to help. They were in almost the exact same spot they'd been standing in when they'd had their confrontation with Gavin.

"I tried, but I couldn't drag her!" Susanna yelled when Stacey approached.

"It's okay!"

Stacey grabbed Angie under her arms and pulled her toward the door. The woman was dead weight, but strength coursed through Stacey's body to get her sister-in-law and friend out.

When she reached the door of the barn another set of hands grabbed onto Angie's middle and lessened her load. Stacey glanced over at Beth and the two dragged Angie several feet away, followed closely by Susanna.

Sirens sounded in the distance, and Stacey turned to see the flashing lights of the fire trucks and police cruisers turning onto the road to their farm.

She smiled and collapsed in the dirt.

EPILOGUE

"Knock, knock."

Stacey turned from her place in the chair and tried to smile as Easton and Detective Reynolds walked into her hospital room.

She'd spent the past three weeks in the hospital being treated for smoke inhalation and burns. Her breathing had greatly improved but the panic attacks she experienced when thinking of that night prevented her from doing too much better. She knew the doctors were worried about her.

Seeing these two together couldn't be a good sign, and she mentally prepared herself for the blow.

"Hey," Easton took a seat next to her and took her hand. "We need to talk to you."

"Did you find Gavin?"

No one had told her anything while she'd been in the hospital. The doctors said she needed her rest and to focus on healing. "Don't think about that night," they'd say. "Just worry about getting better."

It drove her crazy to know everyone else had answers to her questions, and she'd half convinced herself no one would ever tell her the truth. Now, it seemed, the moment had finally come.

"We found his body in the ruin of the house the following morning," Detective Reynolds said as gently as she could manage. "I'm afraid he didn't survive."

A pain shot through Stacey's chest that had nothing to do with her weak lungs. She'd expected this, of course. If Gavin survived the fire in the house, he would have shown up in the barn, but it hurt, nonetheless.

"I figured," she whispered. "That's not why you're here to talk to me, is it?"

"Your sister-in-law woke up today. She'd been shot, hit her head, and suffered smoke inhalation. She's a fighter though. The doctors say she's going to be okay." Detective Reynolds's voice wavered the tiniest little bit. Stacey felt the hesitation there, like she intended to give her as much good news as she could before getting to the point. She didn't have the patience for that.

"Give it to me straight, Detective. After everything I've been through, I think I've earned the truth."

Detective Reynolds nodded her head. "That you have. Alright. We found the girls. There was an underground bunker in the woods behind Gavin's auto shop. One of them is alive, but barely. The others were corpses but all six were there."

Stacey squeezed her eyes. "He said they were alive. I wanted to believe him."

"They had minimal injuries, ironically," Detective Reynolds said. "I believe he didn't intentionally harm them. Cause of death was dehydration. Angie backed this up. In the brief time he had her locked up, she said he brought her food and water regularly, then eventually stopped showing up as our investigation progressed. He became unhinged toward the end, and we believe he lost track of time, forgot to feed and water them. What a way to go."

"I'd like to see the one that survived," Stacey said. "When she's stable. If she doesn't mind."

"I'll ask. There's more I need to talk to you about. Marty and Sherry Randall are completely off grid now. There is no sign of them anywhere, but let me assure you, we are not going to stop searching. They will pay for what they've done. Also, I should tell you David Patterson and his wife have gone back to Boston. Henry Rusher will be going on trial for his crimes with your case, as well as fifteen others."

"What about Susanna?"

"The doctors wouldn't let anyone into yours and Angie's rooms, but Susanna hasn't left. She's been sleeping in the waiting room. Says she can sleep anywhere now." Detective Reynolds glanced at her watch. "I have to go. I have an interrogation to get to, but you know where to reach me if you need me."

Stacey nodded her head, and Detective Reynolds swiftly left the room.

Easton squeezed her hand.

"Listen, Easton. I think with everything that's happened, now isn't the time—"

"I know," he said softly before leaning over to give her forehead a sweet kiss. "I know. It's okay. Do you want me to sit with you?"

"No, but would you mind sending Susanna in?"

"You got it." He gave her a charming smile before leaving the room.

She only waited a moment before Susanna burst through the door and grabbed her hands. "Thank God you're okay. They wouldn't let me in. Said it might upset you. You were in and out the first few days screaming from nightmares."

Stacey sighed. "That explains it, then. I've been begging for information, but they refused to tell me anything."

"Angie's okay. It looked like we were going to lose her. Beth's okay too. She went home to be with her kids, but we told her we'd call as soon as you were allowed to have visitors again."

"Listen," Stacey looked into Susanna's eyes, "I never got a chance to thank you. You saved my life in there. I know it couldn't have easy—"

She'd thought of that moment in the kitchen with Gavin's hands wrapped around her throat a thousand times.

"We saved each other." Susanna smiled and patted her hand. "I know you didn't grow up with me, and I'm a stranger, but I need you to know something. I'm alive today because thinking of you is what got me through. I don't expect you to call me mom. But I would like if you gave me a chance."

"Of course I will."

Susanna wrapped her arms around Stacey, and the two held each other for a moment.

Stacey got to her feet and stared into the unknown. Susanna stood next to her, and Stacey threw her arms around the woman's shoulders.

"I don't know where you are," she said as she stared out the window. "But I will find you. You're going to pay for what you did to our family if it's the last thing I do. So, help me, God. You are going to pay."

Thank you so much for reading! If you enjoyed this book, please consider leaving a review. Reviews help authors be seen, and therefore, make it possible for us to keep making books for readers.

Acknowledgements

There are so many people that made this special book possible. To my amazing beta readers, and critique partners: I wouldn't be here without you. Thank you for all the late-night consults, the kick in the pants when needed, and slugging through the multiple drafts and versions of this book. It was an experience like no other, and the end result is because of all of you.

I want to give a special shoutout to my longest working relationship, my critique partnership with Kat Bethel. Kat, you are an incredible author yourself, and I have enjoyed working with you the past several years. Without your honest feedback and support, this would still be collecting dust in my dresser drawer. Kat read this before all the changes (and before Blackwood Manor existed.)

Thank you to my grandmother and cheerleader, Kathryn Frayne for not laughing at me when I said I wanted to do this. It seems like a small thing, but it did wonders to boost my confidence. You have no idea.

Thank you to my editor Jenny Sliger of Owl Eyes Proofs and Edits for returning to work on this project. Your work is stunning, and I've learned so much from you.

Thank you to my friend Debbie Hyde of D.E Hyde Cover Designs for coming up with the idea for, and creating, this cover. It came together beautifully, and I couldn't be happier with the result. You are amazingly talented!

To my incredible boyfriend, Don, for your patience through the late nights and deadlines; you have no idea how much it means! Thank you for encouraging me to pursue my dreams and supporting me every step of the way. You are my rock and anchor.

Lastly, I can't forget you, dear readers! None of this would be possible without the support and encouragement from every one of you. Thank you for every review, the good and the bad. I'm a better writer because of your important feedback.

Hi there! I'm Ashley Bundy and I'm so happy you picked up my little book baby. I enjoy a good spellbinding mystery, so I thought it would be a good idea if I wrote a few! I like to weave fictional stories with my real-life experiences to make them feel more raw.

The Blackwood Manor duology is based on a couple of haunted houses from my childhood. One was my childhood home, and one was my best friend's. Between the two of us the houses told endless stories. Some of our actual experiences are in these two books, but I'm not saying which ones. You'll just have to guess!! Happy reading!

Where to Find Me

Join my newsletter at: https://ashleybundy.wixsite.com/my-site-1

Facebook: Ashley Bundy Author

Twitter: https://twitter.com/bookloverbundy2

Instagram: https://www.instagram.com/ashleybundyreads/

Tiktok: https://www.tiktok.com/@ashleybundybooks

Goodreads:
https://www.goodreads.com/goodreadscomashley_bundy

Bookbub: https://www.bookbub.com/profile/ashley-bundy

Amazon: https://www.amazon.com/stores/Ashley-Bundy/author/B0CPTG44TK

Miss Blackwood Manor? Find it here
www.books2read.com/blackwoodmanor
www.books2read.com/havenstone

www.ingramcontent.com/pod-product-compliance
Lightning Source LLC
LaVergne TN
LVHW010319070526
838199LV00065B/5604